I'm a single mud
Tyrone an' me li
Dey're me world
an' her princess is
Luv nights out wit me girlos but ye can't beat a
night in wit a bottle of vino an' a masso curdy. I
luv me curdys an' takeaways. We're protected by
de Karma Chameeelion – he watches over me
an' me angles.

HOPE
UR OK
HUN
♥ ♥ XXX

Jules ... # Hope ur ok hun

Kant Kope WITH THE IDEA

OF you BEING SICK.

LOTS OF LOVE,

MARY

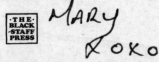

X OXO

First published in 2014 by Blackstaff Press
4D Weavers Court
Linfield Road
Belfast
BT12 5GH
with the assistance of
The Arts Council of Northern Ireland

Hope Ur OK, Hun has asserted its right under the Copyright,
Designs and Patents Act 1988 to be identified
as the author of this work.

Designed and Typeset by KT Designs, St Helens, England

Printed and bound by CPI Group UK (Ltd), Croydon CR0 4YY

A CIP catalogue for this book is available from the
British Library

ISBN 978 0 85640 930 1

www.facebook.com/hopeurokhun
www.blackstaffpress.com

For me angles Tyrone and Rihanna
and de Chinese delivery man.

An' for all de users an' abusers –
de Karma Chameeelion is comin' for yiz.

CONTENTS

QUEEN OF DE NOSEY PASS-REMARKIBELS

So der I am, all snuggled up in me nice comfy bed, havin' some me-time wit a bottle of WKD an' a packidge of King, when outta nowhere I hear dis almighty commotion outside de gaff.

'Ma … Ma … *Ma!*'

Mudder of Jaysus, I tink, me li'l princess is bein' murdered by a chisler fiddler! I leg it down de stairs an' der she is havin' an eppo in de front garden, announcin' to de whole bleedin' world dat she's makin' hur first Holy bleedin' Communion.

'Ma, ye wudn't believe wha' happened in school today! I got a letter off me teacher for me Communion! It has de date an' all de udder tings on it.'

'Shurrup wud ye an' get inside!' I say, takin' de letter off hur. I can't believe she's nearly after givin' me a heart attack for dat! I probably will have a bleedin' heart attack too, de amount I'll be spendin' on dis shite. But d'ye know what? She's me li'l princess of power an' she's worth every penny.

Outta de corner of me eye, I see dat nosey pass-remarkibel Jasinta from number 82 across de road runnin' over in hur housecoat. Jasinta has been livin' in dis estate longer dan I have. De nosey hooer is always at hur window, lookin' tru hur net curtains wit hur beady eyes like a mangy cat lookin' for scraps. She's never out of dat bleedin' housecoat, fag always hangin' out of de side of hur mouth an' ye cud fry an egg on hur head. More grease dan a chipper, de mankbag!

'For fuk's sake, de bleedin' rukshuns goin' on out heyour! What's wrong wit yiz?' she says. She sounds like she smokes sixty Major a day, hur voice is deeper dan de pool in de Fingerless Sports Centre.

'Mind yer own bizness!'

So den she starts mouthin' out of hur, 'Eh, it *is* my bizness when your Rihanna is roarin' an' screamin' out in de middle of de street while I'm makin' de tea!'

An' I'm like, 'Get off me footpath an' get back behind yer net curtains, ye nosey pass-remarkibel!'

Den de durt spits on de ground, calls me a disgrace of a mudder an' legs it back over to hur gaff.

'Like you're ma of de bleedin' year!' I roar after hur. 'Who do you tink you are, passin' comment on me as a mudder when most of your lot are locked up? How's your Keith enjoyin' Portlaoise?'

'Don't you *dare* bring my Keith into dis!' she screams. 'I'd streel outta ye if I didn't have de coddle in de pot!' an' she slams de door.

All bleedin' mouth dat wan, de cheeky geebag. Pot of coddle? Mickeys in water, dat's all dat is. Suits hur down to de ground, de mickey-gobblin' sluh! Well yer gonna get yer kumuppince verdy soon, Jasinta. You just weight an' sea, greasy gumpshuns, weight an' sea!

When I go back inside me li'l prince Tyrone is at de freezer eatin' de bleedin' Viennetta wit his hands.

'Put dat back in de fridge, ye li'l pig feechurs,

3

ye!' I say. 'Dat's for me an' yer Aunty Whitto for our girlo night tomorrow.'

He looks at me like I just trun a bag of cats in de Liffey, ice cream drippin' down his chin. Me prince is a li'l chubmeister. He's always stuffin' his mush. De contrary li'l basturd wuldn't talk to ye for days, but when he's lookin' for his spice bag an' curdy chips he's all over ye like a rash! I do buy him all de best gear from Penney's but all he ever wears is his Adidas trackie bottoms an' a Wolverine T-shirt dat's covered in spaghetti-sauce stains. I tried to trun it in de bin last year an' he fuked de telly remote at me. Didn't try dat again!

'Put dat back in de freezer now, gerrup dem stairs an' finish off yer ekker.'

He truns de ice cream in de freezer, slams de door an' kicks de bleedin' bin.

'If ye kick dat bin again ye won't be gettin' a sniff of curdy tonight!' I say, an' dat stops de li'l fuker in his tracks. De mention of curdy in dis gaff an' I sweyour me li'l angles do be havin' conipshuns. Off he goes up de stairs an' den Ri Ri comes runnin' into de kitchen. I sweyour, I can't get a minute's peace!

'Ma, Ma, I want a tiara an' a masso dress!' she says, an' she starts climbin' up on de chair to get a packidge of me Meanies out of de press. 'When can we go shoppin'?'

'Rihanna, if ye don't calm yerself, yer gonna fall off dat chair an' piddle yer ninnies an' I wont be cleanin' dat off de lino again, do ye hear me?'

'I can't help it Ma, I'm mad exirrah!'

'I know ye are, chicken. It's late-night shoppin' tomorrow night an' we can go to de Lilac Centre.'

'Ah yeah, Ma, nice wan. I want a tiara an' I want new earrings an' I want de biggest princess dress in de whole world! Jazzo was sayin' in school dat she already has hur dress picked out an' it's masso an' Aunty Whitto is lettin' hur get a spray tan an' de eyelashes wit de diamonds on dem. An' she's gettin' one of dem pink Hummers! So I want one of dem too an' a bouncy castle …'

'Jaysus, Ri Ri, is dat all?'

'No Ma, don't be stupid! Kristina in school said she's gettin' a photographer, an' I saw deez deadly cakes wit a Barbie on dem in Thunders so I'll have one of dem, an' ye know de hair

5

extensions in dat shop in Moore Street, de one Aunty Whitto brought me an' Jazzo into last week? I tink de big long pink ones wud be only massive. Oh, an' Ma, can I get dem gel nails wit de French tips, ye know de ones de girls on Tallafornia have? I'm still workin' on me list, it's like Slanty Jaws is comin' again!'

Mudder of divine Jaysus. I shud have known dat little bitch Jazzo would start puttin' ideas in Ri Ri's head – I told Whitto not to let hur watch *My Big Fat Gypsy Weddin'*. I don't know how de fuk I'm supposed to pay for all dis – de Communion allowance has been got rid of an' Ri Ri's da is in de Joy. Even if he *was* here, dat Prik Feechurs basturd would be about as much use as a nun in a hooer house. He'd be sat in de bookies, scratchin' his scrawny hoop an' spendin' his money on de bleedin' horses instead of his li'l princess. Irregardless, I want me princess to have de best Communion ever, so de sky's de limit.

'Alri' chicken, ye can have whatever ye want, but if ye don't tell me what ye want from de Chinese right now yer gonna be havin' Super Noodles for tea.'

'I'm not havin dem Super Noodles, Ma, dey're ascustin'! I'll have curdy sauce, chicken balls an' a spice bag,' me li'l princess says.

'De same for me, Ma, an' I want spring rolls an' chips an' fried rice an' prawn crackers!' Tyrone shouts from upstairs. Me li'l prince comes across a bit tik sometimes but when it comes to de Chinese de li'l pig can hear tru walls.

'Right, yiz li'l hungas, finish yizzer homework an' I'll call yiz down when de food gets here.'

♡ X ♡ X

De next mornin' I get me angles off to school an' send Whitto a text.

✉ HUN: Get ur hoop rownd here 4 a cuppa ♡
✉ WHITTO: K gimme an hour hun xx

Whitto is me younger sister, but she looks about fifty an' she's real immature in comparison to me. Ever since we were kids she's always been de favourite, even when she acted de maggot, an' she always got de heel of de batch wit hur dinner too, de geebag. She was livin' wit Jazzo's da for a few years but dey were murderin' each udder. She turned into dis big stalker weirdo wit him, callin' him an textin' him every five minutes, 'Where are ye?' 'When are ye home?' 'Who are ye out wit?' Non-fukin'-stop.

Turned out he was doin' de durt wit dat bet-down slapper who worked in de Hill. In de end Whitto caught hur wearin' de face off him wit hur hands down his cacks at an Elvis tribute night an' fukin' reefed her up an' down de bar. She trun him out of de house an' told him to clean up his act, but de durty basturd did a legger to Ibeeta an' took dat dopey young wan wit him. Since den, Whitto's put on about twenty stone, grown a ronny an' has started slowly turnin' into me ma. She's always in de same Nike trackies an' dey get more stretched out every day. I do say to hur, 'Ye need more variety in yer diet, get rice wit yer chips when yer gettin' a curdy' an' dat. Does she listen? No. She just eats more chips an' hur face gets hairier every day.

I'm morto when I'm out wit hur on our girlo nights sometimes! I do be dolled up to de nines. Always gettin' de best of de new stock in Penneys.

I do put on me leppard print heels, tube skirt an a top showin' off me diddies. Me gay besto Harley says I'm verdy fashion-forward. He gives me de best tips on choosin' outfits to attract de mickey. 'Hun, yer only massive in dat belly top,' he'll say. 'Dat'd be gorgo wit deez hoopy earrings!' He's like me own personal Gok Wan!

Whitto has no interest in de fashion tho – she does be sittin' der in leggin's or jeans wit hur hair in a pony, lookin' like she's goin' down to pick up hur mickey money from de sowshul! It *does* mean I get me pick of de mickey when it eventually comes our way, but she hardly encourages de fellas to be comin' over to us, dressed like a knacker an' a mush on hur like she's after lickin' piss off a nettle.

She arrives at de gaff wit a pakidge of chocolate digestives. 'What are ye gonna do for de Communion?' she asks while I'm pourin' de tae. 'Jazzo already has me head wrecked lookin' for dis, dat an' de udder.'

'What de fuk is your Jazzo sayin' to Ri Ri?' I ask hur. 'Me li'l princess wants a bouncy castle an' a limo an all!'

'Well, dat's standard, isn't it?'

'Eh, it might be standard but how de fuk am I supposed to pay for it? I'd have to rob a bleedin' bank!'

'What about de Credit Union?'

'I'm not robbin' de Credit Union, ye dope!'

She rolls hur eyes an' dips two chocolate digestives in hur tae at de same time, lickin' de chocolate off first den shovin' de rest down hur gob. Whitto isn't just a muppet, she's Miss Fukin' Piggy hurself.

'No, ye eejit, a fukin' loan!'

'After de last time, Whitto? Are you for serdious?'

De last time I was in de Credit Union der was killin's 'cos I was pretendin' to be me ma to take out a loan . De dopey geebag behind de counter knew me ma from bingo an' rang hur der an' den. I sweyour, me ma must have jumped on hur bleedin' broomstick 'cos in about three minutes she stormed into de Credit Union wit hur coat over hur nightie roarin' at me like I was after murderin' hur bleedin' alasayshun. I didn't see what de problem was meself – de miserable oul basturd doesn't spend a bleedin' penny on anyting. I haven't talked to me ma since, an I haven't stepped foot in dat poxy place – not wit li'l miss 'I'm tellin' yer ma on ye' sittin' der lookin' me up an' down.

Whitto shrugs an' stuffs anudder chocolate digestive in hur gob. 'Well, it's worth a try. C'mon, we better go pick up de girls.'

Whitto tinks de sun shines out of Jazzo's arse, an Jazzo believes hur. She struts around dat school like she's Hannah bleedin' Montana. Always in de best of runners an' de newest tracksuits – she looks like Nike threw up on hur. Spoilt rotten so she is! She's hot an' cold wit me princess too – best of friends one minute, an' den someting better comes along an' she drops hur like a hot snot. She joined de majorettes last September after de Summer Project finished up an' she's been up hur own hoop ever since. I got news for ye, Jazzo – yer not bleedin' Beyonsey, yer just a user an' abuser.

Jazzo legs it out of de school gates an' right up to Whitto's face. 'Maaaaaa, can I go shoppin' wit Ri Ri in town for Communion stuff?'

'Ye have yer majorettes practice, Jazzo,' Whitto tells hur. 'Ye can go shoppin' wit Ri Ri at de weekend.'

Tank fuk for dat! De last ting I want is dat li'l brat windin' up me princess in town. Ye shud see hur at majorettes, trunnin' hur baton at any of de young wans who look sideways at hur.

Whitto heads off down de street wit Jazzo an' de li'l bitch looks back an sticks hur tongue out at me princess.

'Ignore hur, Ri Ri,' I say. 'She's only jello dat yer goin' Communion shoppin' an' she has to go to hur majorettes.'

'I better have a nicer dress dan hur, Ma.'

'Ye will, me princess of power, ye will.'

Wit any luck de li'l geebag will get a smack of a baton an' have a big black eye on de day. If she was a fella she'd be called Damien, de devil basturd child.

So we get on de 40 bus, an' der, sittin' at de back, is none udder dan me fukin' ma. I sweyour – de queen of de nosey pass-remarkibels! Ri Ri legs it down to hur.

'Ah Rihanna, c'mere an' give yer nanny an oul goose gob an' a hug! Where are you off to now?'

'I'm goin' into town to go shoppin' for me Communion wit me ma, I'm mad exirrah!'

12

'Ah, very good, sweetheart! Yer gonna be the most gorgeous girl on the big day, you'll make all the other girls look like muck!'

Me ma looks up at me an' gives me de filthiest look.

'Eh, what de fuk was dat for?'

'Oh, you know quite well, Hun.'

'If yer still havin' an' eppo over dat Credit Union shite den you'd wanna snap out of it an' stop bein' so bleedin' childish!'

'You're a disgrace, I don't know where I got ye from! I only hope me granchislers take after their daddies!' She squints hur eyes at me an' den turns to me princess. 'So, Rihanna chicken, tell me more about your big day – I can't wait!'

I let de two of dem at it an' sit wit me back to dem. De oul wans sittin' in front of us are havin' a good nose, lookin' over der shoulders, pretendin' dey're rubbin' de dandruff off der jackets. Mind yizzer bizness, I tink, an' I give dem filthies till dey turn back around. I sweyour if yiz weren't a hundred years old yiz wud be gettin' a clatter from me!

De oul bag wud never treat Whitto like dis. De golden child! I cudn't do anyting right. 'Whitney did great in school today, got all her sums right. Why can't you be like your sister? You're the eldest, you should be settin' an example! All you do is hang around the laneway like a degenerate, smokin' an' drinkin' ...'

Blah, blah, blah! I sweyour I was sick listenin' to hur. Me da wud stand up for me when he was der an' not in de pub, but eventually he had enough of hur an' ran off wit some prozzy. Eppo fukin' city in dat house when he told me ma he was leavin'!

I do get de odd phone call from him but he never comes over. He's afeared he'll see me ma. He better be comin' to me princess's Communion tho, an' if he brings his prozzy wit him, even better! Dat'll wind up de oul bag.

When we get to O'Connell Street, me ma hugs me princess goodbye, looks at me, an says, 'I'll see *you* later,' wavin' hur finger at me like I'm a bold child. I sweyour, for serdious, I actually kant kope wit dat bleedin' oul wan of mine!

'Ma, can we go to dat masso shop beside Dunnes?'

Der's dis shop in de Lilac Centre dat has de most bewtifel Communion dresses. Ri Ri wants

14

to go tru de Moore Street entrance an' I tink to meself, all dem fordiners wit der hair pieces are gonna be outside der shops an' Ri Ri will be like, 'Ma, Ma, can I have dat one an' dat one an' dat one?' No tanks verdy much! So I tell hur I need to go to Debinims.

'But I don't *want* to go into Debinims!' she screams. 'I wanna go up Moore Street to see de hairpieces!'

'I sweyour if you don't stop yer screamin' yer gonna get de most almighty bleedin' wallop, do ye hear me?'

'Yer a fukin' basturd, Ma!'

Der I am in de middle of Mary Street an' me own daughter calls me a fukin' basturd. All de nosey pass-remarkibels are starin' at me, lookin' me up an' down an' shakin' der heads.

'You only have yerself to blame for that!' says a voice from behind me.

I turn around an' me ma is standin' der wit hur friend Agnes who's tuttin' like she's Skippy de bleedin' bush kangaroo.

'Ma, are you follyin me?'

Me ma starts layin' into me as per usual, tellin' me I'm a disgrace of a mudder, wit

Agnes standin' der noddin' an' sayin' 'Yer right, Betty, yer right!' I turn around to get Ri Ri an' she's legged it. I start walkin' down Moore Street lookin' in all de hair shops tryin' to find hur wit me ma an' Agnes follyin' me an' tuttin'. We stop outside dis shop called Bewtifel Princess an' it sounds like der's killin's inside. Ri Ri legs it out de door wit a clump of hair in hur hands an' de shop assistant chases hur out roarin'.

'You took my hair! You are a child of the devil!' She turns to me. 'Is that your daughter?'

'Yeah, an' wha'?' I say.

'You have a monster for a child. If she was my child she would be spanked and sent to church to ask for forgiveness!'

Is this wan for fukin' real?

'See dis?' I say, an' I stick me middle finger up at hur. 'Swivel on dat an' go back to yer own country!'

Me ma grabs de hairpiece outta Ri Ri's hands an' gives it back to yer wan.

'Sorry 'bout that, love,' she says. 'Me granddaughter has a bit of a want on her.'

Yer wan says someting in fordin talk an'

eyeballs me as she walks backwards into de shop.

Me li'l princess leans in close to me an' whispers, 'Ma, I have anudder one in me pocket.'

I squeeze hur arm tight. 'Not in front of yer nanny, ye dope! Show me later!' I say tru me teeth.

'Right, well, me and Agnes are headin' to The Earl now for a coffee slice and a pot of tae,' me ma says. 'Try not to cause any more ructions. Mind you, I won't be holdin' me breath!' An' dey both give me filthies an' walk off.

I drag me princess into de centre. 'If you call me a fukin' basturd again I'll send ye to one of dem educate togedder schools an' der won't be any Communion for ye! Do ye hear me?'

'Yeah, whatever Ma,' she says, an' she legs it into de shop an' starts doin' laps.

'May I help you with anything in particular?' de shop lady says. She's a right snobby-lookin' bitch.

'Yeah, it's me daughter's Communion in a few weeks an' we're lookin' for de most bewtifel princess dress in de whole wide world. Ah look,

Ri Ri, deez shoes are only masso!'

Sittin' in front of me on de shelf are all deez diamond-encrusted high heels. Dey're just like Ke$ha's shoes. Ye wudn't be leavin' dem shoes on yer windowsill in case de magpies flew down outta de trees an' stole dem on ye! Ri Ri runs over, picks dem up an' looks up at me like she's after gettin' an extra toy in hur Happy Meal.

'Ma, for serdious, I need deez shoes!'

'We don't have those shoes in children's sizes,' snobby nickurs says, rollin' hur eyes. 'Very sorry about that, ma'am.'

'Are you for serdious?'

She looks at me like I'm a leftover bit of kebab sittin' on de side of O'Connell bridge bein' eaten by a seagull. She goes into de back of de shop an' comes out wit deez manky white tings.

'These are the children's Communion shoes that we have in stock,' she says. 'They're sixty euro.'

Dey look like those verookah shoes dat ye wear when yer goin' swimmin' in de pool in de Sports Centre, an' der is no way in hell my princess is gonna be caught dead wearin' dem.

'We need someting wit a heel an' diamonds

18

on dem, luv,' I say to hur.

'Ma for serdious, I'm not wearin' dem. I'd look like a dope!'

'Never mind, chicken, we'll get de shoes anudder time.' I point up at de dresses on de high racks. 'Let's start tryin' on some dresses from de top der.'

Yer wan goes into de back again an' brings out deez awful rags. I've never seen anyting so ascustin' in me life. Real cheap-lukin' material, like de big frilly nickurs ye wud put on a baby when it's bein' christened. Der's no way me princess is gonna look like a mouldy merrang on hur big day, no tanks verdy much!

'This is the affordable range of Communion dresses,' she says.

'What are you implyin'?'

'I just think this range might be more … suitable for you and your little girl.'

Who de fuk does she tink she is? I might not have de money but dat's none of hur bizness! Dis snobby geebag is startin' to rub me up de wrong way. I point up to de biggest, most bewtiful dress in de shop an' I say to snobby nickurs, 'You get dat dress down right now.'

Yer wan says someting under hur breath an' goes in de back to get de ladder. I turn around an' me princess is eatin' a fukin' Mars Bar in de corner an' der's chocolate all over hur hands.

'Did you get yer filthy mawlers all over one of dem dresses?' I ask an' she shakes hur head. I grab hur hands an' spit on dem an' try to rub de chocolate off wit me sleeve. Snobby comes back, ladder under hur arm an' an almighty puss on hur. She puts de ladder up against de dress rack an' climbs up. She looks down where Ri Ri is standin' an' starts havin' an eppo.

'Is that chocolate all over your hands? I'm sorry, but there's no food allowed in here! I'm afraid I'm going to have to ask you to leave.'

Well, me princess starts havin' a conipshun. 'I'm not leavin' here till I try on dat dress!' she roars, 'I am not goin' anywhere!'

Good girl Ri Ri, I tink, you tell hur! Den outta nowhere de mad bitch kicks de ladder an der's an almighty scream outta yer wan as she goes flyin' backwards into de shoe display. I grab Ri Ri by de arm an' say, 'What de fuk are ya after doin', ye eejit?'

Yer wan is moanin' an' groanin' in a pile of

shoes, an' next of all deez two oul' wans come into de shop.

'Little girl, did you just push dat poor woman off de ladder?'

'She did, I saw her do it from across de way!'

I need to get outta heyour. More an' more people are comin' into de shop, an' dey're all whisperin' to each other an' pointin' over at me an' me princess.

'She's unconscious! Somebody call an ambulance!'

Wit dat I grab a veil an' a pair of diamond earrings off de counter an' shove dem in me bag. I push me way tru de crowd an' one of de oul biddies grabs me by de sleeve.

'Yer in big trouble, you are!' she says.

'Out of me way, ye nosey oul geebag!'

We make it outside de shop an' de Lilac Center Security are comin' in our direction. Good ting Ri Ri has a face on hur like butter wudn't melt in hur mouth.

'Get inside Mickey Dee's now an' grab a table,' I tell hur. 'I'll get ye a Happy Meal.'

I'm in de queue an' someone says, 'Ah look,

dey're bringin' in a stretcher! Something's after happenin'.'

I find Ri Ri sittin' at a table wit some li'l girl an' hur ma, helpin' hurself to der curly fries.

'Yeah I kicked hur laddur an she went flyin'!' Ri Ri is sayin' to dem an' laughin'

Tru de window I can see yer wan from de shop bein' carted off on de stretchur into an ambalince. I grab Ri Ri by de arm an' say, 'You keep yer bleedin' mouth shut an' don't be tellin' anyone what happened!'

We sit in Mickey Dee's for nearly an hour until de crowds outside de shop disappear an' dey stop lookin' for us. Den de two of us leg it up to Parnell Street to get de 40 back to Fingerless. I sweyour to good Jaysus me li'l princess is more trouble dan she's worth sometimes! I kant fukin' kope.

Faycebuk Status Update
Hun ders pass-remarkibels evrywere but ye just hav 2 rise above dem no matter how much dey get up yer snot. me lil princess iz me wurld n I wud do anytin 4 hur. shez goin 2 hav de best ov everythin

4 hur communion if I hav 2 sell me hoop 2 mayk it happen ♡ ♡ xxx

---

Like – Comment – Share   👍2   💬9

Whitto hun dnt mind peepl der tiks xx

Hun i no sis h8ers evrywere. fuk dem ♡

Tiffo hope ur ok hun. pm me xxxxx

Hun yeah grand tiffo wan ov dem days ill call ye in a bit ♡

Tiffo ok hun xxxxxxx

Whitto our lil babies r de best in de wurld n dey deserve 2 b treatd like princesses xx

Hun so troo ♡

Tiffo – so troo hun xxxxxxxxx

Whitto – xxx

PRIK FEECHURS

De more I thought about it over de week, de more I thought, fuk, how de bleedin' hell am I goin' to pay for me li'l princess's big day? Whitto has an endless supply of money from Jazzo's da who's in Ibeeta hidin' from de pigs. She's always off spendin' hur durty money on dis, dat an' de udder. New drapes, new settee, new blah blah blah. An' den me ma does be sayin', 'Hun, you should take a leaf out of your sister's book. Look at the lovely home Whitney has to raise Jasmine in.' Shetinks Jazzo's da is workin' on an' oil rig, de tik bitch.

Me only hope in dis difficult time of desperation is Ri Ri's da, Prik Feechurs.

I met Prik Feechurs at an Aslan show in Fingerless years ago. I was standin' at de bar wit Whitto, lookin' like a li'l lash as per usual.

I was wearin' dis masso leather skirt over me best pink leggin's, purple velvet high heels an' a furry waistcoat dat showed off me diddies perfectly. Mickey magnet? Fukin' sure I was. We were drinkin' strawberry an' lemon Woodies. Der was no WKDs in dem days.

Prik Feechurs came over to me an' said, 'How'ye gorgeous, can I fill ye up der?'

'Dat depends, luv,' I said. 'How big is yer mickey?'

Whitto was ascusted. 'I'm goin' to de jacks!' she said.

'Do ye want a biro, luv?' I said to hur.

'For wha'?'

'Yer goin' in der to write yer number on de jacks' walls, aren't ye?'

'Ah, suck on me diddies, ye dope!' an' she stormed off.

Prik Feechurs was verdy charmin', verdy handsome an' by de looks of his pakidge, he had a mickey de size of an elephant's trunk. So I thought to meself, nice wan, I'm gettin' in der. Whitto never came back from de jacks so me an' Prik Feechurs got wasted togedder. We were swingin' out of each udder when 'Crazy World' came on, an' wearin' de faces off each udder at de encore.

'Come back to mine,' he said.

'Wud ye fuk off!'

'Ah g'wan, ye won't be able to walk for days after I'm done wit ye.'

'Well alri' den, on one condition.'

'What's dat?'

'Ye buy me a curdy chips on de way!'

He was right – I wasn't able to walk for days – but not 'cos of his giant mickey. It was 'cos when he was on top of me in de bed de fukin' ting collapsed. I got sick on meself wit de fright of it all, an' de curdy chips came right back up. Me fukin' ankle was sprained an' I was hobblin' around on crutches for de next two weeks. I was never so morto in me life. I wasn't gonna let de kunt away wit dat. I had him runnin' around after me for days – pickin' me up from de gaff, bringin' me down to de Hill, babysittin' me li'l prince Tyrone an' buyin' me curdy chips. It was great.

I wuldn't go near his mickey either. I said, 'You need to earn yer handy shandies pal. Me minge needs a birrah extra attention, d'ye know what I'm sayin'?' He fukin' luved it, de durt.

We were seein' each udder for a couple of months an' it was goin' grand, den one day he said to me, 'I tink ye need to lay off de curdy chips. Yer gettin' yerself a jelly belly.'

'Eh, 'scuze me? What de fuk did you just say?' I was fumin'. Nobody talks to me like dat. 'Ye can go an' take a runnin' jump off O'Connell Bridge, ye li'l gicknah!'

I clattered de fuker in de face, he called me a fat mickey-gobblin' sluh an' we broke up den an' der.

I kept pilin' on de weight over de next few weeks, an' den it turned out I was fukin' preggers. Me jelly belly was me li'l princess Rihanna. As soon as Prik Feechurs found out he was all over me like a rash.

'I'm verdy sorry for sayin' ye had a jelly belly,' he said, 'we can raise our baby togedder.'

I knew I couldn't be dealin' wit dat prick twenty-four-bleedin'-seven, but I'm no fool either. When Ri Ri was born I played de single mudder card an' de corpo gave me a brand new gaff near de village to move me li'l prince an' princess into. I kept seein' Prik Feechurs on an' off for a few years. He was makin' a fortune sellin' ciggies on Moore Street an' he kept us in Penney's best. He was de perfect babysitter too, lookin' after me two angles on Saturday nights while I was out havin' a few scoops wit de girlos. I was livin' de dream, an' den de tik kunt got himself arrested for sellin' yokes outside de Abrakebabra on O'Connell Bridge.

Stupid Lyin' Bastard Feechurs I shud have called him! When de trial came up it turned out he was stickin' his mickey in every gee in bleedin' Fingerless an' buyin' dem all de curdy chips. User an' abuser is all he fukin' was! 'I'm sorry, Hun,' he said before dey put him away, 'I'll make it up to ye, I promise! We'll get married wen I get out an' we can raise Ri Ri an Ty Ty togedder like a proper family.'

'Yeah fukin' right,' I said. 'See ye in five to ten, ye dopey kunt.'

Now I *know* de fuker has money stashed away somewhere. He didn't get arrested for nothin', an I'd bet anyting he has someone mindin' his cash for him while he's inside. So I tink to meself, maybe it's time I paid Prik Feechurs a visit in de Joy.

In de mornin' I get me angles off to school an' hop de bus down to Dorset Street. I walk up to de gates of de Joy an' de pigs search me handbag an' give me de turd agree.

'Who are you visiting today?'

'Me ex, Prik Feechurs.'

'Write down the name of the inmate you are visiting and sign your name at the bottom. You can collect your bag and phone when you leave.'

Oink oink basturds.

I walk into de visitin' room an' it smells like shite. I fukin' hate dis place, it gives me de willies. All de fellas are sittin' wit der wives an' girlfriends, an' dey're all in bits. Greasy heads, no make-up, scabby bleedin' mouths on dem like dey were in a mickey-gobblin' competition at de weekend. I kant actually kope. Den I see Prik Feechurs over in de corner, sittin' der like lord muck wit his mug of tae. He's gone all scrawny lookin'. No curdy chips an' doner kebabs in dis bleedin' place, dat's for sure. I walk over to him an' he looks up an' growls at me.

'Why haven't ye brought me princess in to see me?' he says.

'Eh, nice to see you too.'

'Why are you here? I haven't seen you in months!'

'Our li'l princess of power is makin' hur Communion an' money doesn't grow on trees. Ye need to cough up.'

He looks at me like he's about to fukin' murder me.

'Some piece of work you are! I don't see ye for months an' den outta de blue ye turn up lookin' for money! I've been stuck in here nearly four years, how de fuk do you expect me to pay for de Communion?' he roars at me.

'Don't give me dat shite, I know you have cash stashed away somewhere! Do' ye want our princess to look like a robber's dog on hur big day?'

Wit dat one of de prison guards comes over. 'What's all the commotion over here?' he says.

'Ah nothin', guard.' I say. 'We're just discussin' our daughter's Communion.'

Prik Feechurs stands up. 'Get hur outta here. She's only here to antagonise me!'

'Miss, I think it's time you left,' yer man says.

'I'm not goin' anywhere until dis is sorted out. Dat prick needs to pay his way. You were man enuff to stick yer mickey in me, ye basturd, so now man up an' cough up!'

Prik Feechurs picks up his mug of cold tae an' truns it at me. 'Don't you dare come back here again unless yer bringin' my princess in to see me!' Den de guard grabs hold of him an' starts radioin' for backup.

I sweyour I've never been so morto in me life. Cold tae all over me extensions an' me diddies. Everyone is starin' at me, an' den some cheeky hooer beside me starts laughin'. I turn around to hur an' she gives me filthies.

'What de fuk are you lookin' at?' I say.

'I don't know, but it's fukin' lookin' back!' she says.

'See you, I'm gonna reef outta you outside, ye bet-down slapper!'

'Like to see ye try, ye fat bitch!'

Wit dat two more guards come over, one gets in de middle of me an' dat slapper an' de udder one helps grab hold of Prik Feechurs. Dey drag him out screamin', 'Bring my princess in heyour to see me, ye fukin' bitch!'

'Get me money, ye scabby basturd!' I roar back.

Next of all I'm bein' fuked out of de Joy an' told not to come back until I've calmed down. I'm just lightin' up a fag when de slapper who was startin' on me inside comes out wavin' hur arms an' roarin' at me like she's on Jerdemy fukin' Kyle.

'See you! C'mere an' let's see how smart ye are now ye don't have de guards to protect ye!'

Fuk dat! I leg it down to de road an' flag down a taxi. I get in an' say to yer man, 'Get me to de LUAS red line at Connolly Station an' step on it!'

Yer wan is still runnin' after me screamin'. I roll down de window an' give hur de finger.

'Sorry luv, looks like yer gettin' de tik trayn home! Choo choo, tikko!'

We get to Connolly an' I pay yer man.

'You're a euro short!' de cheeky basturd says, holdin' out his hand to me.

'Verdy sorry about dat,' I say, gettin' out an' slammin' de door.

He rolls down de window. 'If this was my

country you would not get away with doing that!' he shouts.

'Yeah, well if ye don't like it, go back to yer own country den!'

I give yer man de finger as he drives away. Verdy sorry now but I don't have time for dis. I need to get out to de Square to see Harley.

Harley is me GBF – Gay Best Friend. We used to work togedder in Tesco in Phizbrit. De laugh we used to have. We'd be comin' into work hangin' on a Saturday mornin' after bein' in de George all night, knockin' back de WKDs an' gettin' up on de stage givin' it socks. De manager said we were bein' disruptive bein' on de checkouts togedder, an' de bitch put me workin' in de store room. De perverts had cameras in de stock room, an' dey caught me on video robbin' packidges of Meanies, sippin' flagons of cider behind de stacks of pallets an gettin' off wit one of de security guards.

'Yiz have no proof!' I said when dey hauled me up in front of de manager. Dey showed me de footage, had me removed from de buildin' an dat was dat. Pervert basturds watchin' me get off wit yer man on camera! Some people are just ascustin'.

I got preggers wit me li'l prince Tyrone den, an' Harley went off to work in Boots. He's verdy talented at de make-up, does de drag competitions an' all, an' he promised he'd do Ri Ri up for hur big dey. He's masso as well. It's a shame he likes mickey, de li'l lash!

I get out to de Square an' head up to Boots. I walk in de door an' straightaway der he is, 'Heyyyaa Hun!' He's wearin' deez jeans dat are bet onto him an' a sparkly top. Mudder of Jaysus, he's gayer dan Christmas! He legs it over to me an' kisses me twice, once on both sides of me face.

'Yer gettin' verdy posh wit yer two kisses, Harley Reilly!'

'It's sooo nice to see ye, Hun! Oh my Gawd it's been *forever* hasn't it?'

'I know, yer forgettin' about de little people wit dis posho job!'

'Would ye fuk off, ye mad yoke! For reals tho, Hun, yer lukin' masso! Big ridey face on ye! C'mon, I'm on me break now, let's go get a cuppa.'

We head down to de café an' get a pot of tae an' a couple of coffee slices. I fill him in on all de goin's on of de Communion an' Prik Feechurs at de Joy an' all. He says he's verdy excited to be tryin' out some new make-up on me li'l princess. He looks over his shoulder to make sure no one's lookin', then picks up his man bag an' puts it on de table.

'I'm after robbin' all deez new samples, Hun. Ye can go home an' try dem on Ri Ri an den I'll come over de mornin' of de big dey an' do yer li'l princess up proper!'

He empties his bag on de table an' der's millions of tiny lippies an' eyeshadows an' foundations.

'Where's de eyelashes?' I say.

'Ye didn't tink I'd forget about dem, did ye?' he says an' roots around in his bag.

Harley said der were deez masso new eyelashes dat came into Boots, de real long ones wit de diamonds on dem. Me li'l princess wanted dem ever since she saw Hunny Boo Boo wearin' dem on de telly. He takes out de most bewtiful eyelashes I ever saw in me life, real long an' sparkly!

'Me princess is gonna be mad exirrah when she sees dem, Harley!'

'Do ye want a pair for Jazzo too? I have more upstairs.'

'Eh, no tanks verdy much! I'm not doin' dat bitch any favours!'

I start tellin' him about Jazzo an' de way she's bein' goin' on antagonisin' me princess about de Communion.

'De li'l geebag,' he says. 'Dat's shockin'! What if Whitto calls me lookin' for stuff again?'

'Just tell hur yer out of freebies! Eh hang on a second, what d'ye mean *again*?'

'Did she not tell ye? She's already been in to me, an' she brought Jazzo wit hur!'

'Are you for serdious?'

Harley starts tellin' me about last week when Whitto an' Jazzo came out to see him in Boots. Whitto was sayin' dat Jazzo needed to look hur best for de Communion an' cud dey book him for de mornin' of de big day. De cheeky geebag knew verdy well dat I was havin' Harley do Ri Ri's make-up! I tell Harley dat under no circumstances is he to agree to do Jazzo's make-up.

'Well I'll have to tell hur I'm doin' Ri Ri's make-up, Hun. Yizzer gonna be gettin' ready togedder, aren't yiz?' he says in a panic.

'No way! My li'l princess will not be sharin' hur make-up artist wit dat stuck-up li'l bitch. Tell hur nothin', Harley! D'ye not remember Whitto called ye a pillow-bitin' basturd when she caught you an' Seany havin' a ride in de field? D'ye not remember how homerphobic she was? Yer *my* gay besto, not hurs – promise me ye won't say anyting to hur.'

He looks up to de heavens, shakes his head, lets out a big sigh an' den agrees.

'Harley, yer a ledgebag. I'll buzz ye later anyway, I'm headin' over to Tiffo's now for a curdy an' a sneaky bottle of veeno!'

Tiffo's been me besto ever since we were small – we were in first class togedder. She had just moved schools an' she walked into Mrs Kennedy's classroom on de first day tinkin' she owned de place. Hur hair was in a big high pony wit one of dem giant scrunchies an' 'cos she was new she didn't have hur uniform for nearly two weeks, so every day she was comin' into school wearin' a new outfit. I remember one of de girls in de class sayin' to hur, 'Heyour, you look real common!' She turned round an' punched de li'l geebag in de face. From dat point onwards we were stuck at de hip. I played piggy beds wit hur in de school yard an' we started havin' sleepovers every week. We were mad for de *Moon Dreamers* an' *She-Ra*. I even wanted to call me princess She-Ra when she was born, but Prik Feechurs had an eppo as per usual.

I remember when me an' Tiffo made our Communions togedder. We went to Captain America's after de church, it was deadly. Me ma never liked Tiffo, an' she hated hur even more after dat. Said she was a bad influence.

'I don't want you hangin' around with that Tiffany any more,' she told me. 'That young wan is nothin' but trouble! She caused ructions in the church, she swore at the photographer – and I think I saw her stealin' from the tip jar in the restaurant! You're not to be playin' with her any more, d'ye hear?'

Ma couldn't stop us tho. She got into a big fight wit Tiffo's ma one day. Told hur dat we weren't suited as friends an' dat it was best we didn't play togedder any more. Well, Rita took one look at hur an' told hur exactly where to go, an' she was right! Rita was de better mudder by far – she adored Tiffo an' always told hur how proud of hur she was. De only ting my ma ever said to me was, 'Why can't you be more like Whitney?'

Den me da wud look up from de paper an say, 'Betty, wud ye shut fukin' up an' leave de chisler alone! Wudn't it be worse if she had no friends?'

He was always stickin' up for me like dat. I cudn't have asked for a better da. I don't blame him for leavin' me ma – I don't know how he put up wit dat pass-remarkibel geebag in de first place!

Tiffo still lives at home wit hur ma, in Fatima Manshuns. Dey're verdy posh livin' on de south side. When I get to de house I ring de bell an' I can hear dat mad fukin' dog dey have start barkin' an' scratchin' at de door. Wuff Wuff dey called it. Serdiously, fukin' Wuff Wuff! Dey sound like terrible dopes when dey're callin' him. 'Wuff Wuff, get in heyour!' dey do be roarin' out de window. Gas basturds.

'Who is it?' Rita says tru de door.

'Rita, it's me!'

'Ah Hun, c'mon inside!' she says as she takes de door off de latch. Wuff Wuff is havin' a fukin' eppo.

'Get inside, Wuff Wuff, ye stupid fukin' mutt, ye! Let hur come in!'

'How'ye Rita, are ye alri'?' I say as I squeeze me way tru de crack in de door. Wuff Wuff is jumpin' up all over me. I don't know what kind of dog he is but his paws are de size of a fukin' sofa an' he smells like soggy cornflakes. Ye know, like when ye stik de bowl in de microwave to heat dem up when de evenin's get cold.

'Ah I haven't seen ye in ages, Hun, give us an oul' hug!'

I go into de kitchen. 'D'ye want a bit of coddle, Hun? I just made it. I saved de heel of de batch for ye and everyting!'

'Gerrup de yard, Rita, yer verdy good tinkin' about me an' de batch. I'm de size of a fukin' house tho at de moment, all de bread I'm eatin'.'

'Sure look at de size of me here! Me apron only fits over one of me diddy didos!'

Rita is as big as a house. She's always in hur apron an' she has dat purple hair dat ye do see de mad oul wans comin' out of Peter Marks wit. Der's always a smell of dinner off hur. I don't tink she ever leaves dat kitchenette!

'Where's Tiffo?'

'She's upstairs dyin' her hair again! It'll be fallin' out of her head next. Silly bitch has it a different colour every week – she tinks she's dat Lady Goo Goo wan off de telly.'

'I'll be down in a minute! I can hear yiz talkin' 'bout me!' Tiffo roars from upstairs.

Rita puts de coddle down in front of me. Fukin' bowl of mickeys. I can't eat dem. I just dip me batch heel in an' eat it wit a bit of brown sauce.

'Wuff Wuff, get out of de bin an' stop eatin' dem badayta peels, ye stupid bleedin' dog!'

Wuff Wuff looks up at me wit a bit of badayta peel hangin' out of his mouth an' when Rita turns to de cooker I trun him a mickey from de coddle. Next ting Tiffo comes thumpin' down de stairs.

'She's like a baby bleedin' effalent!' Rita says, givin' me a wink, which is more like a blink 'cos she can't do it wit one eye. Mad oul wan.

'How'ye Hun!' Tiffo says an' gives me a hug.

'Tiffo, what bleedin' colour is yer hair?'

'It's fire engine red, Hun, why?'

Me an' Rita look at each udder.

'Your hair is gonna fall outta your head, ye mad bitch!' Rita says.

'Shurrup Ma an' mind yer own bizness. At least it's not purple like your bleedin' mop!'

Rita just tuts an' starts wipin' down de counters wit a J-cloth.

'So c'mere Tiffo, will ye come shoppin' wit me in Charlestown tomorrow? I need to look for a tiara an' some udder jewellery for Ri Ri's Communion.'

'No probs, Hun, I don't have to be in de sowshul 'til de afternoon.'

I fill Tiffo in on all de goin's on wit Whitto an' Jazzo an' der poxy Communion plans. She tinks Whitto is an' awful fukin' dope an' agrees wit me dat Jazzo is a bleedin' devil child, so she's well on for gettin' one up on dem. I do feel terrible sometimes givin' out about me own but Jaysus knows dey drive me to it.

'Right me lovies, I'm off to me leaba. I'm only fit for de knacker's yard.'

'Night Rita.'

'Night Ma.'

Rita folds up hur apron, hangs it over de cooker handle an' goes upstairs.

'Don't feed dat dog any sausies out of yizzer coddles. De little basturd will be fartin' out of him all night,' she roars down from de landin'.

Wuff Wuff looks up an' barks at me. He sleeps in de bed wit Rita every night, but wit de amount she eats I'd be more worried about de dog dealin' wit hur farts dan de udder way round.

Tiffo rolls hur eyes. 'She's such a sap!'

'Leave yer ma alone Tiffo, ye don't know how lucky ye are wit hur. She's bang on – unlike my bleedin' oul wan.'

'Is she still given ye grief, Hun?'

'Every fukin' day, I don't even answer hur calls anymore. But me angles do have me tormented to go up an' see hur. She treats dem like Egipshun Fairohs.'

'She's been a real kunt to ye since yer da left. I remember when she wasn't dat bad.'

43

'Eh yeah, in de lettin' on days.'

Tiffo starts laughin'. 'C'mon an' we'll get a curdy chips from de Chinese. Ma's coddle is muck, has me fartin' an' all. I don't know what she bleedin' puts in it.'

'Yeah, I'm not one for turnin' down a mickey but I can't eat a full bowl of boiled ones.'

We head down to de Unlucky Dragon an' get a couple of curdy chips an' a portion of chicken balls an' sit on de wall outside eatin' dem.

'Hun, listen to me, ye know I luv de bones off you an' Ri Ri, don't ye?'

'Will ye stop, ye soppy fuker!'

'No Hun, I'm bein' serdious. You've always been me besto, an' ye know I tink de world of Ri Ri. De day you asked me to be hur godmudder was one of de happiest days of me whole life! I sweyour to Jaysus, I'll be doin' everyting I can to help make dis Communion de bestest day ever for Ri Ri!'

'Ah Tiffo, yer verdy good. Now give over will ye. Ye know I don't do all dat soppy shite!'

Tiffo laughs. 'G'wan den, I'll see ye in de mornin', righ'?'

'Alrigh'. Don't be feedin' any more mickeys or

badayta peels to Wuff Wuff or yer ma will have a fukin' Dutch oven in hur room tonight.'

'Wud ye fuk off, ye mad bitch!'

Tiffo, yer only gas.

Faycebuk Status Update

Hun sumthymes ur real family r not ur actual family n ur real family r just nosey pass-remarkibel basturds ♡ ♡ xxx

---

Like - Comment - Share   👍 2   💬 8

Whitto wat de fuk does dat mean hun xx

Hun nuthin im not talkin bowt u ♡

Whitto eh i hope yer not xx

Hun im not in de humour ov u 2nite verdy sordy but fuk off me page ♡

Whitto r u talkin bowt ma? xx

Hun i told ye im not in de humour now jog on sis ill ring ye 2mordo ♡

Tiffo luv u hun, c ye 2moro xxxxxxxx

Hun xxxxxxxx ♡ ♡ xxxxxxxxxx

DE KARMA CHAMEEELION

✉ HUN: What time am I meetin ye ?♡
✉ TIFFO: 10 hun is dat alrite? xxx
✉ HUN: Sound see ye outside de frunt door ♡

Wit me li'l basturds gone off to school, I get into me best trackies, de pink Joocy Cutehooer velour ones wit de diamonds on de hoop of dem, an' head down to Charlestown shopping centre. It's fukin' lashin' out of de heavens. When I get to de centre, Tiffo is standin' just inside de door havin' a smoke an' some fordiner is givin' hur grief.

'It's rainin' fukin' cats an' dogs, I'm not goin' out in dat! I'll smoke where I bleedin' want to, righ'?'

I walk closer an' I can hear yer wan givin' out stink in hur big tik accent. I sweyour, I don't know how she expects people to understand hur!

'I just cleaned this floor,' she's moanin'. 'There's a no smoking sign right there! I am not here to clean up after the likes of you my whole day. Stand outside if you are smoking please!'

'De likes of me? What de actual fuk?'

De cheeky fukin' bitch. Who de hell does she tink she is talkin' to me hunzo like dat? I walk right up to dem an' gerrup in yer wan's face.

'Heyour, who de fuk do you tink you are talkin' to hur like dat? Where de fuk are you even from?'

'I'm not going to take this abuse. Smoking inside is breaking the law. I'm going to get security!'

'Gwan den, off wit ye! An' go back to yer own country while yer at it!'

She moves back an' legs it off into de centre squintin' hur eyes at me, de hooer. Tiffo hands me a smoke.

'Dey have some cheek, don't dey?'

'I know, Hun, comin' into our country, stealin' our jobs an' den actin' like dey own de fukin' place.'

Tiffo's on me wavelength. We have all de same opinions.We're like sisters. In sayin' dat, I am far better lookin'. Tiffo has a deadly sense of style an' all, but she looks verdy slutty. I, on de udder hand, dress for de mickey but in a verdy subtle way. If we were Spice Girls, Tiffo wud be Gerrup-On-Me-Now Spice an' I'd be Ye-Can-Have-A-Shot-Of-Me-Gee-After-Ye-Buy-Me-A-Curdy-Chips Spice. It's all about de tease, not givin' it up at first glance. De two of us togedder tho? Mickey magnets!

'Are we gonna get pancakes before we start shoppin', Hun? I'd mill an' eclair as well.'

'Ah I forgot it was panky on de chubby dey! Let's go into Thunders, dey always do a luvly panky in der.'

We're walkin' in de direction of Thunders when next of all, who do I see only Jasinta Pass-Remarkibel from number 82. I'm leggin' it over to de sports shop to dodge hur but she spots us an' starts waddlin' over in our direction. I sweyour dis oul wan is like a dose of de crabs – fukin' impossible to get rid of.

'Heyour Hun, Hun! C'mere, I wanna talk to ye!' Jasinta roars from de udder side of de shoppin' centre.

'Who de fuk is dis mad oul wan?' Tiffo asks me, lookin' Jasinta up an' down. She's shufflin' hur way over to us like she's dyin' to go to de jacks, an' she looks like she dressed hurself out of de Vincent de Paul clothes bin. She's wearin' a Celtic hoodie, a black knee-length skirt wit hur slip nearly down to hur ankles an' a pair of white Nike runners wit brown tights. She has dem mad chicken legs wit a jelly belly. Like an egg on bleedin' legs! De hairs on hur legs are stickin' tru de tights an' all. She looks like she shud be sellin' de *Big Issue* on O'Connell Street.

'I'm sorry, Jasinta, but I can't talk to ye right now. I'm shoppin' for me princess Ri Ri's Communion an' I'm verdy busy.'

'Just a second now, Hun, I thought you might be interested to know dat I was down in de fishmongers earlier an' yer wan dat works der had a lovely bit of smoked coley put aside for me, but she had to shut up de shop an' throw out all hur fish 'cos some young fella had trun a stinkbomb an' half a dozen eggs into de shop.'

'An' eh, why exactly are ye tellin' me dis?'

''Cos de oul wan in de shop said it was yer pride an' joy, Tyrone!'

I grab hur by de hood of hur Celtic top, reef hur to de side an' push hur against de wall. Verdy sorry now, Jasinta, I tink, but you've passed one too many comments on me angles. Ri Ri an' Ty Ty, dey're me world. Jasinta is most certainly not me world, but she has a fukin' way of pushin' herself in de middle of it half de bleedin' time.

'Dis is just me havin' a little word in yer ear to be given ye a bit of fair warnin'!' I say, gettin' right up in hur hairy face. 'You talk about my angles like dat again an' I'll be trunnin' ye off de bridge onto de M50, d'ye hear me?'

'De apple doesn't fall far from de tree wit your lot, does it? Yer a disgrace of a mudder so ye are. Get yer bleedin' hands off me!'

'D'YE HEAR ME?' I roar, twistin' hur greasy mop.

'Yeah, yeah, I hear ye, I hear ye! Now get off me, ye mad kunt!'

'Der will be a knock at your door one of deez

days, Jasinta. Knock knock!'

'Wha'?'

'KNOCK KNOCK!'

'Eh ... who's der?'

'De Karma Chameeelion, KUNT!'

'You're a freak! Get off me before I call de security!'

I let go of hur an' she scarpers off wit hur tail between hur legs like a dog after gettin' a boot up his hoop. Tiffo is standin' der laughin'. 'Ah Hun, yer gas.'

'I know. Now c'mon an' we'll get our pankys.'

We order our pankys, wit a couple of milky teas an' a sliced turnover for me tea later an' den we get on our way. I need to get a masso tiara for me princess so she looks like a real princess on hur big day. Tiffo says der's a shop dat sells de most glamorous costume jewellery an' we shud try der for someting a bit sofisterkated. Nothin' less for me princess of power.

We walk up to de shop an' I'm nearly blinded by de sparkles. We're wanderin' around just havin' a nose an' I notice yer wan behind de till keeps lookin' at us out of de corner of hur eye.

''Scuse me, how much is dat?' I say, pointin' at one of de tiaras.

'It's 65 euro,' she says without takin' hur beady eyes off us.

'Do ye do hire purchase?' Tiffo asks.

'No.' An' she crosses hur arms an' squints.

I sweyour to Jaysus, I'm startin' to tink dat every fukin' shop assistant in de country is lookin' down der nose at me. We carry on walkin' around for a few minutes, lookin' at all de bewtiful earrings an' brooches an' bracelets, an' yer wan is like a mirror – no matter which way we turn, she's standin' der in front of us wit a face on hur like a donkey's arse.

'Eh, I'm verdy sorry, but do we have a problem heyour?' I say.

'I beg your pardon?'

'Don't give me dat,' I say. 'Yer follyin' us around like a moggy in heat, yer so far up our holes!'

'I'm very sorry, Miss,' she says wit an ascusted look on hur face. 'I was just wondering if you needed any assistance.'

'Alri' den, giz a look at dat tiara der – not de 65 euro one, de big one beside it. How much is dat?'

She takes de keys out of hur pocket an' unlocks de counter. She points an' says, 'You mean this one?'

De tiara is mahoosive, just like a real fairy princess crown. Three red rubies at de front an' six points on de top wit a diamund on each one. She takes it out of de case an' holds it up for us.

'This one is one 145 euro,' she says.

'Dat's verdy expensive! Do ye do discounts at all? It's for me li'l princess's Communion.'

'No, I'm afraid we don't.'

'Can we try it on?' Tiffo says, reachin' for it.

'Yeah, give it heyour!'

She verdy reluctantly hands de tiara over to us. Tiffo goes to grab it an' de ting slips out of yer wan's hand an' goes flyin' across de shop floor.

'Ah verdy sorry 'bout that, I'll get it!' Tiffo says.

Yer wan leans over de counter. 'No, no, I'll get it, leave it where it is, please! Leave it where I can see it!'

'Eh, 'scuse me, are you tryin' to accuse us of someting?' I ask hur.

'Yeah, what d'ye tink we are?' Tiffo says.

'Common fukin' thieves?'

Next of all dat fukin' cleaner appears outside de shop wit dis mahoosive security guard.

'That's them!' she says, den she points at Tiffo. 'And that's the one who was smoking inside!'

I turn around an' while yer wan is lookin' for de tiara Tiffo is takin' jewellery out of de unlocked case an' shovellin' it into hur pockets. De security guard points at us an' roars, 'Here, you two! Don't fuckin' move!'

Dat's our cue to run! We leg it out of de shop an' toward de main exit.

'We forgot de turnover, Hun!' Tiffo says. I look back over me shoulder an' yer man is leggin' it after us an' shoutin' into his little radio, pantin' like a dog on a hot day an' sweatin' like a priest in a playground!

'Forget de bleedin' turnover, Tiffo, yer after gettin' caught rapid ye fukin' eejit!'

Next of all Tiffo trips over hur wedges and lands face-down on de ground, an' all de earrings an' brooches an' rings she's after nickin' are scattered all over de tiles.

'Tiffo, ye dope, get up!'

Dat fat fuker security guard is catchin' up wit us. Tiffo's tryin' frantically to gather up all de jewellery an' shove it back in hur pockets. I pull hur up, an' de dope is so busy lookin' over hur shoulder at yer man dat she runs gee-first into a bench.

'Me fukin' gee!' she roars.

At dis stage der's nosey pass-remarkibels everywhere starin' us out of it an' I'm fukin' morto. I reef Tiffo up by de collar.

'Never mind yer gee or de jewellery, we're gonna get ourselves arrested if you don't fukin' move it!'

'Me fanny is broke!' she moans, an' I drag hur limpin' sideways out de front foor.

When we get outside der's a taxi waitin' at de curb. De driver rolls down his window. 'Philomena?'

'Yeah dat's me, we're goin' to de village,' I say, hooshin' Tiffo in de back seat. 'Me mate's after breakin' hur gee so ye better step on it!'

He looks at me wit his gob open. 'Eh, right so. The village it is.'

I jump in de frunt just as de fat fuker security guard comes runnin' out de frunt door, sweat pourin' off his baldy head.

'Move, mister taxi driver!'

I roll down de window an' stick me head out. 'Fuk you, ye fat wanker!' I shout, an' I give him de jippo hand.

'I've reported you both to the guards, they know who you are!' he shouts, wipin' his forehead wit his sleeve.

'Yeah whatever, swivel on dis ye sumo obese basturd!' an' I give him de finger. De driver heads down towards de village an' Tiffo is still in a hoop in de back of de car whingein' about hur fanny.

'Hun, serdiously, me gee is broke. I need to go home an' stick a packidge of frozen fish fingers down me nickurs.'

'I need to go see Lemmy about gettin' me princess a limo for hur Communion. Heyour mister driver, drop me off in de village first wud ye? Yer wan in de back is goin' to Fatima Manshuns.' De taxi driver leans over to me an' whispers in me ear, 'Are you sure she doesn't need to go to the hostipal love?'

'Ah she's grand, it's not de worst ting she's ever done to hur gee!' I say, an' I crack up laughin'.

Tiffo doesn't see de funny side, de grumpy bitch.

♡ X ♡ X

Lemmy used to own dis manky car repair place in de village dat me brudder worked in. I tink de whole bizness was just a front for someting 'cos I don't tink dey ever had a single customer. De place wud be empty an' de two of dem gee-eyed after fallin' out of de pub in de village. De two of dem used to run riot around Fingerless togedder.

After me brudder went to Portlaoise Lemmy sold de bizness an' bought a couple of limos and set up in a new place next to de chipper.

All de little girlos in Fingerless want Lemmy's pink Hummer limo for der Communions an' Confos. When me princess saw it outside one of de gaffs on de estate she turned to me an' said, 'You better get dat fukin' limo for me Communion, Ma, right?'

'Watch yer language, ye li'l shit, I'll see what I can do for ye,' I said. Cheeky fukin' bitch tinks I'm made of money.

Lemmy comes out de frunt door beside de chipper, trackie bottoms an' a jumper on him. He has a big hairy mole on de side of his face. It looks like it's sproutin' bleedin' mushrooms! He's bald on de top an' has a giant combover. His fingernails are ascustin' too, all long an' yellow like he never heard of fukin' nail clippers.

'Ah Hun, c'mere an' give us an' oul gooser,' he says, an' he leans in an' wears de cheek off me. Close yer bleedin' mouth, ye durt bird, I tink, I can feel yer tongue all over me face.

'How'ye Lemmy, what's de story?'

'Ah ye know yourself, just keepin' me head above water. Keepin' me head above water.'

He has a bit of a stutter on him an' he says everyting twice. It's verdy annoyin'.

He tries to squeeze a hug out of me den. I sweyour, I tink all he wants is a feel of me diddies. He was always letchin' off me, swingin' outta me anytime I was in de pub drinkin' wit me brudder, tryin' to get me to dance wit him when 'Maniac' came on.

'C'mon upstairs, Hun, c'mon upstairs to

me office. I believe yer li'l Ri Ri is makin' hur Communion.'

'Dat's right, Lemmy, an' she wants de pink Hummer for hur big day.'

He opens de door an' waves his arm for me to go in. 'Ladies first, ladies first!'

Stop fukin' repeatin' yerself ye weirdo. I walk up de stairs an' turn around an' der he is, havin' a good oul goo at me arse.

'Are ye enjoyin' de view der?'

'What's dat, Hun?'

'Nothin'.'

We go into his office. De place is tiny an' de smell of young fella wud make ye heave.

'Crack open a window, Lemmy, will ye?'

He opens a window an' sits down on a manky armchair behind what looks like an old school desk. I'm standin' der tinkin', is he for fukin' real? De inside of de Hummer better not be in a hoop as well.

'Sit yourself down there, love. Now tell me, what date is de Communion?'

I give him all de details an' he tells me de date is available.

'How much is it?'

'For you, Hun, I'll do a verdy special discounted price of 100 euro.'

'Ah Lemmy, dat's verdy expensive. Can ye not bring dat down a bit for an oul pal?'

'Dat's de lowest I can go, love, honest. I have other requests for dat day an' I'd be chargin' dem a lot more. I'll give ye first refusal tho, how's dat sound to ye?'

First refusal? What does dat even mean? He looks me over an' says, 'Do ye want a cuppa while ye have a think about it?'

'G'wan den – three sugars, two tea bags an' loads of milk.'

'Right.'

He walks over to de kettle, sticks it on to boil an' says 'I need a 50 per cent deposit upfront an' ye can pay de rest on de day.'

Fifty fukin' yo yos? De robbin' basturd. I have a quick look tru me purse when he isn't lookin' an' come up wit 5 euros an' 63 cents. I can't let me princess down tho. De Hunzo charm is gonna have to come out in full force for dis fuker.

I tiptoe over to de desk an' sit up on de edge of it while Lemmy's pourin' de tae. I cross me legs real serductivley an' pull me trackies down a bit so ye can see a li'l glimpse of me G-string. Lemmy turns round wit a mug of tae in his hand an' his eyes nearly pop out of his fat head.

'Jaysus Hun, I have to say, yer lookin' well since de last time I saw ye. Lookin' real well so ye are …'

'Curves Lemmy, an' de Zumba. Keeps me verdy fit.' I say in me most serductive voice, an I lean in toward him an' squeeze me diddies togedder. Me fun bags are fukin' huge ever since I had Ri Ri an' I might as well put dem to good use. Lemmy is proper gawkin' at me, an' he's startin' to stutter again.

'Eh, eh – how many sugars did ye say ye wanted, Hun?'

'Two big wans, Lemmy,' I whisper, leanin' in furthur, 'two *real* big wans!'

Lemmy's face goes bright red an' his hands start shakin'. De poor sap is getting' all aflustered. He's tremblin' so much he dribbles tea all over his shirt an' down his trackie bottoms. I slide off de desk an' lean over to him, me diddies in his face.

'D'ye need a hand der, Lemmy? Yer after

spillin' tea all over yer clothes …'

'D-d-dat's okay, H-hun. I have it under c-c-control ...'

I grab him by de jumpur an' give him a look dat cud turn Harley straight.

'Are ye sure ye don't need me to help ye … take deez off?'

De dopey fuker looks like he's about to faint. Dat shud do it, I tink, an' I grab him under de chin an' look him right in de eye. 'I'll leave ye to clean yerself up. Put me down for dat date for de pink Hummer. I'll sort ye out wit payment some udder time. Right?'

'R-r-right Hun, sure ting … I'll eh, talk to ye …'

'Ye will, babes, ye will for sure.'

I wipe a li'l dribble of tea off de mug, look Lemmy in de eyes an' lick it off me hand as I walk out de door. De fukin' dope, as if I'd go near him wit a barge pole! Show a fella yer diddies an' a sneaky peek of yer durty mind an' I sweyour, ye can get away wit blue murder.

✉ WHITTO: Were r u? i pickd up
   tyty n riri from school der in
   de hill wit me xxx
✉ HUN: sound ordur me a wkd ill
   b der in 5 ♡

When I get to de Hill Ri Ri legs it over an'
swings hur arms around me.

'Ma, Ma, guess what? Guess what?'

'What is it, me li'l princess of power?'

'Jazzo is after gettin' a photographer for hur
Communion! Can I have one too? Please, Ma?'

'I can take dem on me phone Ri Ri, ye don't
need one.'

'But Maaaaa!'

I can see Jazzo sittin' der beside Whitto all
smug, de little shit. It's well for fukin' some.
Just wait until dey heyour about de pink
Hummer.

'I have a surprise for ye, me li'l princess,' I say
as I walk over to de udders.

I sit down beside Whitto an' take a sup of me
blue WKD. 'Nice wan, Whitto, I'll get ye back.'

'Where were you? Took you ages to get here,'
she says.

'I, eh, went to see a man about a dog,' I say

wit a wink.

'We're gettin' a dog, Ma? Is it an alasayshun?' Ty Ty looks up at me from his Gameboy ting.

'No, ye dope. I was bookin' de pink Hummer limo for Ri Ri's Communion.'

'Ah Ma, are ye for serdious?' Me li'l princess says an' she leaps up off de chair an' hugs me round de neck.

Whitto turns around to me wit a verdy jello look on hur puss. 'Ah verdy good. Where from?'

'Lemmy.'

'Wha'? I asked him de udder day an' he said he'd get back to me.'

'He will, an' he'll be tellin' ye it's not available.'

Jazzo turns round to Whitto wit a devious expression on hur face. 'Ma, you better get a pink Hummer limo for me. I want to be like one of dem girls from de Playboy mansion when I'm arrivin' at dat church.'

'I'll sort ye out, don't worry, chicken.'

Den Jazzo takes a piece of paper out of hur school bag.

'Dis is me list of tings I want for me Communion an' me ma is gonna get dem all, aren't ye, Ma?'

She hands me de list an' mudder of fukin'
Jaysus de child has thought of everyting.

✿ Me list for me Communion ✿
by Jasmine, age 8

Masso princess dress
Pink Hummer limo
Tiara wit loads of pink diemunds
Eyelashes wit de kristals on dem
Santra pay spray tan
High heels wit de ribbons goin up de legs
A deadly DJ
Red lemo an choklit biskits an sambos an
   cupcaykes an chips
Silk gluves
Diemund earings
French manicurd nails

I shove de piece of paper back into hur schoolbag
so Ri Ri doesn't see it an' start gettin' ideas. I'm
not rubbin' me diddies in anyone else's face an'
I'm not bein' chased by any more sumo obese
security guards, no tanks verdy much.

'Enough of dat now,' I say, 'get yizzer homework done while me an' yer ma have a few scoops.'

'Can we get a curdy after?' Tyrone says.

'Finish yer ekker an' den we'll see, right?'

'I want chipper Aunty,' Jazzo says, 'I don't like Chinese.'

Fukin' bitch.

Dey finish off der ekker an' Whitto starts tellin' me about Jazzo's majorettes competition next week. I'm like, yeah yeah, whatever. Li'l bitch in hur sparkly leotard trunnin' hur baton all over de place, I can't fukin' wait. I tink I'd rather pull de mickey off Lemmy while lickin' milky tae off his face.

As she's mouthin' out of hur I'm startin' to panic. How de fuk am I gonna pay for dis Communion? Once Ri Ri sees dat list, der'll be no stoppin' hur – she'll want everyting Jazzo is gettin' an' de rest, an' I sweyour to Jaysus me li'l princess will be wantin' for nothin' on hur big day!

I'm tinkin' back to what Whitto said about tryin' de Credit Union, an' at dis stage, it's either dat or I start givin' hand shandys on

Benburb Street. I like de mickey but not dat much! If I wear a bit more foundation an' put me hair up dey might not recognise me at dat Credit Union. An' if dey do, den fuk dem. Fuk dem, an' fuk me ma, de nosey pass-remarkibel basturd! You just weight an' sea!

Faycebuk Status Update
Finglas Neighbourhood Watch [In conjunction with Finglas Garda Station]

There was an incident today at the local shopping centre at Charlestown. Two females were seen shoplifting from Twinkle Jewellery Store but unfortunately had left the premises before security arrived. The two individuals were in their late twenties/early thirties, and were in sports wear. Witnesses described the women as 'very rough' in appearance. If anyone has any information regarding these individuals please contact us on this page or at the local Finglas Garda station. Thank you.

Like – Comment – Share   👍 1   💬 2

Tiffo ruff? ill giv ye fukin ruff wen I find out out who runs dis page n smash yizzer windits in xxxxxxx

Hun yiz kan go n ask me slyce, de state ov yizzer faycebuk page n de hack ov dat shoppin centur its full ov fordiners. its like a box ov lego, its in bits! ♡

USERS, ABUSERS AN' FORDINERS

I wake up wit de mudder of all headaches to an almighty racket.

'Ma, wake up! Ma!' Ri Ri is hoverin' over me in de bed an' roarin' at me.

I jump up an' der she is in hur pull-ups an' hur school shirt lookin' like she's been dragged tru a hedge backwards.

'Ye li'l fuker, yer nearly after givin' me a heart attack!'

'Ma, Tyrone is eatin' frozen chips for his breakfast again.'

I luv me li'l prince but he's a fukin' dope, bless his cotton socks. He'll eat anyting he can get his hands on if der's no Pop Tarts left.

'Will you put some ninnies on over yer pull-ups an' go brush yer hair, ye look like a wino. I'll go sort out dat brudder of yours.'

I drag meself out of bed an' down de stairs. Tyrone is in de kitchen rootin' tru de freezer. De presses are all open an' der's empty packidges everywhere. I sweyour, he's like Slimer from *Ghostbusters*.

'Tyrone!'

He turns around to me wit his hands behind his back an' wit crumbs an' Jaysus knows what else all over his face. 'Ma, der's no Pop Tarts.'

'Are you eatin' oven chips out of de freezer again?'

'No, Ma, Rihanna is just bein' a kunt an' tellin' lies.'

'You watch yer fukin' language! What are you hidin' der? Show me yer hands!'

I grab him by de collar of his shirt an' turn him round an' sure enough he has de bag of frozen chips behind his back.

'Mudder of Jaysus Tyrone, I don't know what de fuk is wrong wit you. Yer gonna give yerself cramps again an' I won't be sittin' up all night tonight boilin' 7Up for ye! Now put dem back in de freezer, dey're for yizzer tea later.'

I look up at de clock an' it's after nine already. I sweyour de li'l gicknahs are always late for school. I shout up to Ri Ri an' she comes downstairs wit a brush in hur hand.

'Will ye brush me hair, Ma?' she says, an' I start unknottin' it. De child has a head on hur like a brillo pad. She's yelpin' out of hur an' complainin' at me when me stomach turns an' I drop de brush.

'Rihanna, der's creepy fukin' crawlies in yer hair!'

'Oh yeah, me teacher said der's nits goin' around de school. She gave us dis yesterday,' an' she hands me a piece of paper outta hur shirt pocket.

Dear Parent or Guardian,

This letter is to inform you that an individual in your child's class has head lice.

Though bothersome, head lice will not harm children or adults, nor cause illness, and do not indicate that a person is unclean or their environment is dirty. Head lice are almost always transmitted from one child to another by head-to-head contact, and so are very common in a primary school environment.

If an inspection reveals that your child does have lice, you should treat by combing to remove the adult lice and using a medicated shampoo or lotion in order to treat the nits. We recommend 'Be Gone

With You!' which is a pyrethrin-based lotion available from the local pharmacy. Special metal or plastic lice combs, such as the LiceMeister, can also be found in the pharmacy.

If you have any concerns or queries regarding this letter or your child, please do not hesitate to contact either myself or the school liaison officer Sister Immaculata, on the school's main phone line. Alternatively you can make an appointment with the school secretary to speak with either one of us.

Yours sincerely

Miss Blathnaid Murphy

(2nd Class Teacher)

Dat durty fukin' school. It's all dem manky children, spreadin' der diseases an' der creepy crawlies. It's a wonder me li'l angles don't come home wit worse.

'Tyrone get over here an' I'll check yer hair.'

'For wha'?'

'Nits! Now c'mere!'

Me prince comes over to me an' I have a look tru his mop. It doesn't look like he has anyting crawlin' around his head, tank Jaysus. I grab two baseball hats out of de press in de hall an' stik one on Ty Ty's head an' den I put Ri Ri's hair up into a bun.

'Ma, yer hurtin' me head!'

'Shurrup de fuk.'

'But Ma!'

'But nothin'!'

I stick two clips into de bun an' put de baseball cap on Ri Ri's head.

'Now listen to me de two of yiz. Don't be takin' dem off yizzer heads until ye come home, an' if de teachers say anyting tell dem I told ye to wear deez in class 'cos of de nits from de durty children.'

'But Ma, I feel stupid in dis hat, it's bleedin' dopey-lookin".'

'I don't care! Keep dat on yer head, d'ye hear me? I'll get some of dat nit shampoo today an' sort yiz when ye get home from school later, right?'

De two of dem nod der heads wit faces on dem like slapped arses. I give dem each a packidge of Meanies for der breakfast an dey head out de door whingin' an' moanin'. Li'l basturds.

I rinse me hands wit Toilet Duck an' start gettin' meself ready to head down de Credit Union. If dey recognise me I'm fuked – dey told me never to come back after de last time – an'

I'm just wonderin' how de fuk I'm goin' to pull dis off when I remember de bag of make-up samples Harley gave me. I empty de whole lot onto de kitchen table an' go to work. I lash on a No7 foundation dat's three shades darker dan me face wit loads of bronzer on me cheekbones, paint on some sparkly blue an' green eyeshadows an' draw me eyebrows right up on me forehead wit a black eyeliner. To top it all off I put on some bright red lipstick an' tie a leppard print scarf round me hair like an oul one goin' to Mass or one of dem Arabian women. I check meself out in de mirror. I look like a fukin' dope, but hopefully a dope dey don't remember.

I dig me Credit Union book out of de cutlery drawer. I haven't used it in years an' de bleedin' ting is covered in Chef sauce or someting. As I head out de door, I look over at number 82 an' see de net curtains twitchin'. Nosey basturd Jasinta is der sittin' in hur armchair an' peekin' out de window at me like a pervert. I pull de scarf down further over me face an' try to get away before she sees de state of me.

I don't see anyone I know on de way to de Credit Union, tank Jaysus, an' der's only two people in de queue in front of me. Of course der's only one person behind de counter, an' de oul wan dat's bein' served is rootin' tru hur little granny trolley lookin' for someting.

'Cud ye go any slower?' I mutter under me breath, lookin' round to make sure de security guard hasn't recognised me yet.

Someone comes in tru de security door an' joins de queue behind me, an' I sweyour, de smell of sherry an' brussel sprouts wud knock ye out. Der's a tap on me shoulder, an' when I turn around who is it only Jasinta Pass-Remarkibel hurself. I sweyour to Jaysus de basturd folleyed me down here.

'Der ye are, Hun,' she says, gawkin' at me like a fukin' turkey. 'I was wonderin' where you were off to dis mornin'.'

'Jasinta I'm startin' to tink you must be a lezbean, 'cos yer stalkin' de hoop off me de past three days!'

'I'm only here to make a payment, yer just paranoid! What are you here for? An' what's wit yer make-up?'

I'm tinkin' I'd love to deck de nosey bitch but I don't want to draw attention to meself, so I turn

75

me back to hur an' start goin' tru de forms on de counter beside me: Payment Plan, Insurance, Opening a New Account, Loan Request. I pick up de Loan Request form an' start fillin' out me name.

'What's yer loan for?' Jasinta says, leanin' over me shoulder to get a look.

'Wud you ever fuk off an' mind yer own bizness!' I say under me breath. 'Did ye not get de verdy clear message I gave to you yesterday?'

De oul wan ahead of me finishes up at de counter an' I leg it up to de glass an' trun me form tru de hatch. De quicker I get away from dat pass-remarkibel bitch de better. Yer wan behind de glass stands up an' says, 'Sorry love, I'm just on me break now, someone will be with you in a sec!' I can practically feel Jasinta smirkin' at de back of me head. Next of all, who comes out to take hur place only Evelyn, de same nosey oul wan who ratted me out to me ma de last time. I pull me scarf down over me eyes an' tink, fuk, I shud have worn sunglasses as well, 'cos dis bitch will see right tru me.

'Now, how can I help you?' she says as she looks up at me. Hur eyes open real wide for a sec an' den she squints at me tru hur glasses.

'What's your name again? I know you don't I?' she says.

I shake me head an' shove de form in front of hur lookin' down at de ground. She stares at me, poutin' hur lips an' frownin'. 'You're Betty's daughter, aren't you?'

I say nothin'. She opens me Credit Union book, takes one look at me name an' says, 'You are Betty's daughter, I *know* you are. You needn't try to fool me, and you needn't start causing trouble here like you did last time!'

'Listen, I'm not here on me ma's behalf dis time, alrigh'?' I say, pullin' de scarf off me head. Fat lot of good dat did me. 'I have me own account an' I want to take out a loan.'

'Do you have ID?'

Why is she askin' me for ID if she already knows who I am? De tik bitch.

I give hur me sowshul card an' she starts typin' someting on de keyboard an' glancin' over hur shoulder at de security guard. She has a face on hur like thunder. I turn around an' Jasinta is tryin' so hard to eavesdrop she's practically up me arse. She looks at me den jumps back in de queue an' starts fiddlin' wit de application forms.

'What is this loan for?' Evelyn asks.

'Me daughter Rihanna's Communion,' I tell hur.

She squints at de computer screen an' looks up at me. 'You have no money in this account. You cannot take a loan out with no money in your account.'

'If I had money in me account I wudn't be lookin' for a loan wud I? Ye dope.'

'I'm afraid you don't quite understand how a credit union loan works,' she says wit a smirk on hur face, 'you can take one of our information leaflets if you would like to learn more about – '

I slam me hands down on de counter an' press me face up against de glass. 'Listen you, dis is me daughter's Communion we're talkin' about an' I am not goin' *anywhere* until I get me loan approved!'

She just smiles at me an waves over de security guard.

'Is everything okay, Evelyn?' he says. Big muscley fuker wit a head on him like a bowlin' ball.

Evelyn shakes hur head an' points hur fingur at de door.

'Verdy sorry now but dis is victimisation!' I say to him, 'I am bein' refused a loan for no reason!'

'Madam as I have already said, you need to have money in your account to take out a loan,' Evelyn says. 'John, please escort this lady out. She's being very disruptive and there's a huge queue building up behind her.'

Den Jasinta waddles up to de counter. 'Is everyting okay, Hun?' she says.

I push hur away from me, spittin' wit anger. 'Don't you come near me! I warned you yesterday!'

Wit dat de security guard grabs me by de arm, 'You'd better leave.'

I try to push him off me but he's fukin' huge an' his hands are like bleedin' vice grips.

'Dis is assault!' I shout. 'Gerroff me!' At dis stage de whole room is starin' at me an' whisperin'.

Evelyn picks up de phone. 'Right, that's it. I'm calling the Gardaí.'

'I'm leavin', I'm leavin'! Calm yer nickurs.'

I turn around to Jasinta who is smirkin' away an' say, 'You weight an' sea, ye prick, folly me again an' I'll end ye!' De security guard leads me out de door, an' I give dem all de finger tru de window.

I'm lightin' up a fag an' tryin' to wipe some of de make-up off me face when me phone starts ringin'.

'Hun, I'm stuck in de bookies 'cos Georgina hasn't showed up for hur shift!'

Typical Whitto. De bitch only calls me when she's lookin' for a favour. 'Yeah, so?'

'I need ye to bring Jazzo to hur majorettes practice after school.'

'I'm verdy sorry now, but I don't have time. I have to go to de chemist to get nit shampoo an' scrub de kids.'

'Here, I have to go, I have a customer. Majorettes practice starts at four o'clock. Tanks Hun, I owe ye a WKD.'

Den she hangs up. Fukin' dope. Like I don't have me hands full already wit me own walkin' disasters.

I stop into de chemist on me way to de school. Yer wan behind de counter looks up an' smiles so hard I can see all hur molars.

'Oh hi there, how can I help you?' she says.

'Oh hi yerself,' I say, lookin' around to make sure der's no one listenin'. I lean in over de counter. 'I need de nit shampoo,' I whisper.

'I'm *so* sorry, could you repeat that?'

'I said I need de nit shampoo!' I say louder, an' some oul wan shoots me a durty look from de jam rag section.

'Oh, you mean for head lice?'

'Nits, I said nits! Me li'l princess has nits. Do ye want me to tell all of bleedin' Fingerless while I'm at it?'

'Oh my God, I am so sorry, I just couldn't hear you properly. Bear with me one second, now, we have a couple to choose from.'

Yer wan goes rummaging around de shelves an' comes back to me wit two different bottles.

'Now, we have this one called "Licey Not Nicey", which is an overnight lotion, and this one is "Be Gone With You!" and that's a rinse-out shampoo.' An' den she starts chucklin'.

'Eh, excuse me, but do you find it amusin' dat my daughter has creepy crawlies in hur hair?'

'Oh goodness no, not at all. It's a terrible nuisance when our little angels bring those itchy head-beggers home from the classroom! I just think the product names are *so* silly, don't you agree?' An' she starts gigglin' to herself.

I think dis wan is takin' a few of de tablets from de shelves in de back, de bleedin' weirdo.

'Dat one,' I say, pointin' to hur right hand, 'dat's de one de school told us to buy.'

'No problem at all. That's €16.49 when you're ready.'

'Does de medical card cover dis?'

'I'm afraid not. Is there anything else I can help you with today?'

I take de money out of me purse an' hand it over to hur. 'No, if I bought anytin' else from ye I'd be broke.'

As she puts it tru de till I reach me hand down, grab a packidge of johnnys from de counter in front of de till an' slip dem in me handbag.

She hands me back me change an' smiles, sayin' 'Have yourself a great day!'

'Ah, wud ye fuk off.'

She stares at me wit hur gob open as I walk out de door. Robbin' basturds in dat chemist. At least I got some rubbers out of it. Two for de price of one – gerrup de yard!

I walk down to de school an' I'm a few minutes early to pick up me angles an' de devil child. I go inside to de office an' de speccy-eyed receptionist is der behind de window. I knock on de glass an' she looks up at me.

'I want to talk to Miss Murphy or Sister Immaculata,' I say. 'I'm Rihanna's ma.'

'You'll have to make an appointment. Let me just see when they're available …'

She looks down at hur diary, flips tru de pages an' says, 'Miss Murphy will be free on Thursday at 10 a.m., Sister Immaculata will be taking the class for Communion prep at that time.'

Speccy has deez big tik jam-jar glasses dat take up half of hur face an' a massive mop of curly red hair. If Bosco an' Deirdre Barlow ever had a ride de end result wud be dis stuck-up fuker.

'I tink it wud be better if Sister Immaculata blessed de heads of all de kids in de class so dey don't have bleedin' nits anymore.'

Speccy stares at me tru hur bottle-caps wit dis blank look on hur face an' says, 'I'll pencil you in to see Miss Murphy on Thursday at ten, so.'

De bell rings, an' I'm about to leave when I notice a sign stuck up next to de window.

***** 4th 5th & 6th Class Boys Sports Day *****

WHERE? - St Assumpta Park, off the Village Roundabout

- FEATURING -

Three-Legged Race ✻ Egg and Spoon Race ✻ Relay ✻ 5-a-side Football

And much more!

WHEN? - Wednesday 24 April

First Event Begins at 10 a.m.

Please ensure you sign the permission form that was sent home with your child and that you return it no later than 17 April.

Each child needs to have the following on the day:

PE Gear (Tracksuit, comfortable sports shoes)
Change of clothes
Bottle of water
Packed Lunch

All parents are encouraged to attend.

Let's Get Fit, Let's Have FUN!!!

An' I'm tinkin', me li'l prince is in fifth class an' he never told me about dis. Egg an' spoon race, for serdious? Is dis de fukin' eighties?

'What is dis sports day all about? My Tyrone never brought any note home to me.' I say to Speccy.

'The notes were sent home last week. I can give you a new form now to sign if your son has lost the original.'

She hands me a form an' I fill it out an' scribble me signature across de bottom.

'Will you be in attendance?' Speccy asks when I hand it back to hur.

'I always cheer me li'l prince on at his sports days. He's verdy good at de sprints.'

'We need some parents to volunteer. I'll put your name down for that then, shall I?'

'I, eh …'

Before I can answer hur she's scribblin' my name down in hur diary an' tellin' me I need to be there for nine to help set up. She hands me a list of jobs for volunteers an' I'm already regrettin' openin' me big gob.

SPORTS DAY PARENT
VOLUNTEER LIST

On the day you will be asked to help out with:

- Distribution and collection of sporting equipment before and after each event

- Filling up water bottles and ensuring children are kept adequately hydrated throughout the day

- Refereeing of matches and races

- Keeping all children safe and in the appropriate groups when they are not participating in a sporting event

For fuk's sake, dis is de last ting I need. A day in de poxy rain in de poxy park wit udder people's poxy fukin' kids.

'Great, tanks for dat,' I say tru me teeth, an I try to leave before I get meself roped into anyting else.

'Oh could you be a dear?'

I wasn't fukin' quick enough! 'Wha'?'

'Can you hard-boil four dozen eggs the night before and bring them with you for the egg and spoon race?'

'Eh …'

'Lovely stuff! See you then!'

Fukin' bitch!

De kids are pourin' out tru de corridors an' next ting I see Jazzo skippin' down de hall, spinnin' hur baton an' swingin' hur hips an' singin' at de top of hur voice like she tinks she's Shakira. Me princess is walkin' along behind hur wit hur finger stuck up hur nose. Fukin' eejit.

'Ri Ri, get yer finger out of yer nose!' I roar at hur.

She hasn't got de baseball cap on hur head. I sweyour to Jaysus.

I pull hur away so Jazzo can't hear us. 'Where's dat hat I put on you dis mornin'? I told ye to keep it on!'

Den all of a sudden she starts bawlin'. 'Ma, de udder kids in my class are basturds. I hate dem an' I want to change school! One of de boys was callin' me creepy crawly head an' ripped de hat off me when de teacher wasn't lookin'.'

Me poor princess of power. Li'l basturds in dat class gave hur dem durty nits an' now dey're givin' hur jip over it? I almost forgot how hordible kids can be.

I wipe Ri Ri's tears an give hur a hug. 'Yer a verdy brave girl, me brave li'l princess. When we get home tonight we can get curdy chips an' have cuddles on de settee an' watch de Kardashians, okay?'

She nods an' whimpers into me chest, gettin' snot all over me Joocy Cutehooer hoodie.

'Where's yer brudder?'

'He got detention, Ma.'

'De li'l bollix. What did he do?'

'I dunno, but he won't get out till five o'clock.'

Jazzo is swingin' hur baton an' watchin' hur reflection in de glass of de school noticeboard. I roar over to tell hur dat I'm takin' hur to majorette practice.

'Whatever Aunty, I don't care who takes me,' she says, puttin' hur hands on hur hips an' poutin' at hur reflection. Cheeky li'l geebag.

'Heyour, why didn't you stand up for Ri Ri in class today when dey robbed hur hat?'

She shrugs hur shoulders at me an' den marches out de front door, twirlin' hur baton an' kickin' hur legs, Ri Ri eyeballin' hur from me arms.

De majorettes practice is in de parish centre a few minutes from de village. Whitto says dat all de mudders dat do be der are snobby dickheads, always tryin' to out-do each udder. As we walk into de hall der's a line of of dem sittin' on de benches wit der li'l girls, all brushin' der hair an' fixin' der outfits an' as we walk by dey all stare at Jazzo. De mudders are all turnin' to each udder an' whisperin', de nosy pass-remarkibels, an' de girls have faces on dem like rabbits after seein' a fox. I'm here tinkin', I don't know what dis wan's been up to but by de looks of it she has rubbed deez fukers up de wrong way an' has got herself a serdious reputation for bein' a li'l devil child.

De troop leader turns around an' when she sees Jazzo hur face goes pale

'Dis is me Aunty,' Jazzo says to hur, pointin' at me wit hur baton.

'Point dat ting at me again an' I'll shove it down yer throat,' I whisper in hur ear, an' she drops it.

'Oh, there's been a bit of a mix-up ...' yer wan starts sayin' to me, an' she tells me dat Jazzo isn't needed for dis practice.

'This is only for the group routine,' she says to me. 'Jasmine has a solo in the competition so we're going to be running through that first thing at nine o'clock tomorrow morning.'

'I'm after comin' all de way down heyour, are you for real?'

She pulls me to one side an' whispers to me, 'Jasmine is much more … advanced than the other girls, so she doesn't really need to be here for the group run. She will be front and centre for the competition – the other girls will just be following her lead. There's a little bit of, shall we say, animosity between her and the other girls so really I think it would be best to do a one-on-one rehearsal with her.'

Animalosity? Wha'? 'C'mon den Jazzo, yer comin' back tomorrow. Ye can come home wit us til yer ma finishes work.'

We walk back out tru de hall, passing all de mudders an' daughters on de way, an' one of de mudders mutters someting under hur breath. I walk over to hur an' say, 'What did you just say?'

'Nothin', I was just talkin' to my little girl,' she says, lookin' me up an' down.

'I shud hope so.'

'Excuse me?'

'You heard me! Keep yer comments to yerself. Yiz are just jello because Jazzo is more talented dan all yizzer brats put togedder.'

We walk out of de hall an' outta nowhere Jazzo grabs hold of me hand.

'Tanks for standin' up for me, Aunty,' she says wit a big grin on hur face. I'm like, is dis wan for real?

'Eh, whatever,' I say, pullin' me hand away from hur. 'Yer ma was right, de mudders in der are all nosey pass-remarkibels.'

I turn around an' Ri Ri is scratchin' an' pickin' creepy crawlies out of hur hair. I sweyour to Jaysus, I actually kant kope wit deez li'l basturds sometimes.

'Come on you two,' I say, 'curdy an red lemo for you an' a few WKDs for me.' Mudderhood is verdy rewardin', but sometimes it's a massive pain in me hoop.

Faycebuk Status Update

Hun do i luk lyke a bleedin robber r sumthin? made a bleedin show ov in dat poxy smelly kredit union 2dey. ill rob yiz de next thyme. showur ov basturds

♡ ♡ xxx

Like – Comment – Share 👍2 💬6

Tiffo wats wrong hun? Wat happened? Xxxxxxx

Hun dose fukurs wudint giv me a loan n de snotty fukur behind de cowntur had me trun out. it waz discrimnerashun ♡

Tiffo ah hun call me in de morning. dnt mind dem der de wans dat luk like robbers dogs xxxxxx

Hun tnx luv ♡

Whitto ma wants 2 talk 2 u xx

Hun she kan talk 2 me hoop ♡

TIK TRAIN BASTURDS

✉ HUN: Jazzo wasnt needed 4 de praktis. u hav 2 bring hur down 2 de hall 2moro mornin b4 de competishun. ill bring hur 2 back 2 mine n get a curdy 4 dem ♡

✉ WHITTO: right hun tanx ill come up 2 ye after work xxx

I bring Ri Ri an' Jazzo back to de gaff an' find Tyrone sittin' on de settee watchin' de wrestlin' on de telly wit his hand down his jocks.

'Heyour, what did you get detention for?' I say.

'I trun a chair at Micko Ward, he said you were a sluh,' he says.

'Good lad, Ty Ty. We're orderin' from Hai Wun. What do ye want?'

De hungry pig feechurs starts listin' off his

order an' I write it down. I ask Jazzo an' me li'l princess what dey want an' add it to de list. Jazzo is moanin' out of hur dat she doesn't like de Chinese food, but I tell hur she'll get a clatter if she says dat in my gaff again an' dat shuts hur up.

'Now go wait in de livin' room wit Tyrone while I'm doin' Ri Ri's hair – an' put down dat fukin' baton! If ye break anytin' I'll break yer face!'

She legs it inside to Tyrone an' de two of dem start fightin' over de remote. I pick up me phone an' ring de Hai Wun. I sweyour it's de best curdy in Fingerless. We do call it de Hai Wun heroin. It's masso.

'Three cups of curdy sauce, one spring roll, large portion of chicken balls, one chicken fried rice, one chicken chow mein, two chips, three spice bags an' a portion of prawn crackers ... Half an hour? Sound.'

Ri Ri is drinkin' red lemo out of de bottle in de kitchen. I grab hur an' de nit shampoo an' go upstairs to de bathroom.

'Ma, I don't want to put dis stuff in me hair. Kristina in school said it smells ascustin'!'

'I don't care what it smells like, yer not stayin' in dis house wit creepy crawlies in yer hair. Now get yer head over dat sink.'

Me princess moves hur head over de sink an' I take de lid off de shampoo. Muddur of Jaysus de smell *is* fukin' ascustin'. Ri Ri starts whimperin' an' squirmin' an' I grab hur head.

'Keep still, dis will only take a minute!' I say. I run de water over hur hair an' start to squeeze out de shampoo. De smell is so bad it's makin' me vurp, I can taste de chicken fillet roll I had for lunch. I hold me breath an' rub de shampoo into Ri Ri's hair an' she starts roarin'.

'Ma, stop, yer gettin' it in me eyes! It's stingin' me, Ma!'

She starts bawlin' hur eyes out, an' when I look down der's a stream of piss tricklin' down Ri Ri's leg an' onto me fukin' slipper. For fuk's sake, she's after piddlin' hur ninnies! I squeeze de rest of de bottle on an' start scrubbin' hur head.

Next of all Jazzo walks into de bathroom.

'Why are yiz all screamin'? Me an' Tyrone can't hear Hunny Boo Boo on de telly,' she says.

'I thought I told you to wait in de sittin'

room!' I say, tryin' not to breathe in too much of de smell.

'Ma, I sweyour, I'm gonna get sick if ye don't let me up!' Ri Ri is sobbin'.

Jazzo takes one look at hur an' de li'l bitch starts smirkin.

'Eh, it's only shampoo,' she says, 'don't be such a bleedin' baby Ri Ri!'

At dat, Ri Ri starts havin' a fukin' eppo. She jumps away from de sink an' grabs Jazzo by de neck. Der's suds an' water flyin' an' de two of dem are swingin' out of each udder an' wreckin de bathroom. Ri Ri starts rubbin' de shampoo in Jazzo's face an' de li'l bitch starts bawlin'.

'Ahh, Aunty, get it off me – me eyes are stingin'! Dis smells ascustin'!'

'Wud yiz give it fukin' over!' I'm roarin, tryin' to pull dem apart. 'Yiz'll have me house ruined!'

'Where's me ma? I want to go home!' Jazzo is wailin', an' den she starts rollin' around on de tiles an' retchin'. I reef hur up by de armpits.

'Get yer bleedin' head in dat toilet if yer gonna get sick. D'ye heyour me?'

'Ma, what's dat smell?' Tyrone is shoutin'

from de bottom of de stairs. 'Does Ri Ri have de skuts again?'

'Don't come up heyour, Tyrone, stay in de sittin' room!'

De gobshite comes upstairs an' sticks his head into de bathroom. Ri Ri is sobbin' over de sink, Jazzo has hur head down de jacks, an' der's nit shampoo all over de walls.

'What de fuk is goin' on?' he starts shoutin'. 'For serdious, what's dat smell? It's ascustin'!'

I pick up Ri Ri an' put hur in de bathtub still bawlin' hur eyes out. 'Ma, will ye get dis out of me hair now? Pleeease, Ma!' I grab Jazzo an' trun hur into de tub as well. I turn de shower on an' rinse de two of dem down head to toe, de durty mankbags. Tyrone is standin' der starin' like a tik an' diggin' his nails into his bleedin' scalp.

'Tyrone, why are you scratchin' yer head?' I say. He looks at me like I'm fukin' nuts.

''Cos it's itchy, ye tik bitch!' he roars at me. 'Why else would I be scratchin' me bleedin' head?'

'Don't you dare speak to me like dat ye basturd!' I say, an' I pull him over to get a look at his head. It's full of bleedin' creepy crawlies.

'Ah Ma, yer not gonna put dat shampoo in me hair, are ye?' he says.

'Der's no way I'm goin' near dat shite again,' I say, 'now get yer head over dat sink, Tyrone, yer gettin' a haircut.'

'No Ma, fuk off. I like me hair de way it is.'

I reef him by de arm. 'Yer gettin' awful cheeky, ye li'l basturd! Get yer head over dat sink now! D'ye hear me?'

He starts tuttin' an' whingin' out of him an' he shuffles over to de sink. I reach into de bathroom cabinet an' get out me ladyshaver an' go to work on his head.

'Now me li'l prince, ye look like one of dem Gee-eye Joes!'

He gets up an' looks in de mirror. 'Ah Ma, dat looks bleedin' rapid!' he says wit a big grin on his face.

Next ting de doorbell rings. De fukin' Chinese is here.

'Stay where yiz are, de three of yiz!' I say, an' I go downstairs an' open de door. De Chinese fella stands der gawkin' at me wit his mouth wide open.

'You okay, lady?' he says.

'What de fuk is dat supposed to mean?' I say, an' den I look down. Me T-shirt is drenched an' stinkin' of nit shampoo an' puke, an' der's clumps of hair from Tyrone's head stuck to me diddies. I trun de money at yer man an' take de food. Nosey pass-remarkibel basturd.

Next ting I see Whitto come tru de garden gate. She stares at me an' starts sniffin' de air. 'What happened to you? An' what de fuk is dat smell?'

'Come an' see for yerself!'

De two of us go upstairs. Ri Ri an' Jazzo are sittin' in de bathtub, both still bawlin' der eyes out, an' Tyrone is checkin' out his new baldy head in de mirror. Whitto hovers outside de jacks wit hur sleeve coverin' hur face.

'Right,' I say, 'get yizzer clothes off you two, we need to boil dem!'

'De smell of dat fukin' shampoo, Hun, mudder of Christ!'

Whitto takes Jazzo out of de tub an' wraps hur up in a housecoat. I rinse de rest of de shampoo off Ri Ri's an' she won't stop snivellin'.

'Shurrup wud ye!'

'But *Maaa*!'

'But nothin'! Shurrup!'

I grab anudder housecoat out of de hot press an' wrap hur up in it. We take de three of dem downstairs an' divvy up de Chinese. I have to give Ri Ri extra chicken balls an' red lemo to make hur stop cryin', de li'l gicknah.

I tell Whitto about de incident earlier wit de majorettes leader an' de pass-remarkibel mudders. She tells me dat's been goin' on since Jazzo got de solo in de competition an de udder girls were all verdy jello of hur.

'Someting's gonna happen tomorrow, Whitto, you just an' weight an sea,' I tell hur. 'Der's gonna be killin's!'

'Ah don't be silly, Hun, it'll be grand. I'd better get madam home in anyways. Big day tomorrow, she needs hur bewty sleep!'

'Ye can borrow some of Ri Ri's tings to bring hur home in. I'll disinfect all de clothes before I see ye tomorrow.'

Or trun dem in de bin, I tink, de fukin' smell off dem.

She dresses Jazzo in one of Ri Ri's tracksuits

an' brings hur home. I've never known de child to be so quiet. You'd sweyour she was traumatised.

'Right yiz li'l basturds, time for bed. Yer goin' to yer nanny's in de morning an' den we're all goin' to de majorettes competition. Now, gerrup dem stairs!'

Off dey go. I'm dyin' for a bit of me-time after de day I had. I grab a WKD from de fridge, a packidge of Banshee Bones from de press an' bundle meself up in me duvet on de settee. I luv me-time, der's nothin' like it. Feet up, angles in bed, an' de *Eastenders* omnibus on de telly. Nice wan.

> ✉ TIFFO: hun did ye heyour about
> de communion stuff der sellin
> in aldi? X
> ✉ HUN: no!! r dey sellin it in
> de 1 down de road? ♡
> ✉ TIFFO: no hun only de 1 on
> parnell st me ma got a flier
> 2day when she was in town.
> meet me in anns on mary st 4
> brekkie @ 9 2moro n we can
> head round X

De next mornin' I drop me angles round to me ma's an' head into town to meet Tiffo for a fry. Few sausies an' rashers an' a bit of white puddin', fukin' luvly. She shows me de flier dat hur ma got in Aldi. Dey have dresses, veils, gloves an' shoes an' even de rosary beads. I'm tinkin' to meself, dis cud be de answer to me prayers. Aldi does be verdy good value.

'We shud get a move on, Hun, I'd say de queue is a mile long already. Dey're only goin' on sale dis mornin'.'

We walk around to Aldi an' Tiffo's right, der's a mahoosive queue goin' right all de way down Parnell street. I ask dis oul wan in de queue what de story is, an' she says dey're just bringing de stock in off de truck now an' dey'll be open at ten.

'I'm hopin' to get some nice accessories for me granddaughter,' she says. 'Some gloves an' a veil an' dat. She'll be only delighra!'

'Yeah whatever, I didn't ask for yer life story,' I say.

Tiffo hands me a smoke an' we light up, tryin' to figure out what to do next. She says de fella she was seein' before Christmas used to work here an' on his lunch break dey used go down de laneway where de loadin' bay was an' she'd give him a quick hand shandy. De durt.

'I think I remember where it is, Hun, de truck might still be der! C'mon down heyour wit me.'

We start walkin' down de side of de buildin' an' der's a smell of piss an' der's used rubbers all over de ground. Can't believe de durty bitch used to be pullin' dat fella off down here. We walk around de corner an' der's de truck, still bein' unloaded. Bingo! A fella climbs out of de back of it carryin' a bundle of white dresses all wrapped in plastic.

'What are you girls doing here?' He shouts over at us. 'This area is staff only.'

'We're lookin' for Vlad!' Tiffo says. 'Is he in der?'

'Hold on now an' I'll see.'

Yer man walks into de loadin' bay an' me an' Tiffo leg it over to de back of de truck. Tiffo clasps hur hands togedder an' bends down to give me a hoosh up. I take a runnin' jump up an' she yelps.

'Jesus, you've put on weight, Hun!' she says, wincin'.

'Wud ye fuk off!'

I get inside de truck an' der's fukin' tonnes of stuff – dresses, veils, gloves, rosettes, I've hit de fukin' jackpot! Gerrup de yard! I start goin' tru de dresses tryin' to find a nice wan dat wud fit me princess when Tiffo sticks hur head in de back.

'Hurry up, Hun, I tink dey're comin' back!' she whispers at me.

'Keep dem occupied will ye? I need a few minutes.'

'Are ye takin' de piss? Get a fukin' move on. I don't want to see Vlad an' yer gonna get caught rapid in de back of dat fukin' truck!'

Next ting hur head disappears an' I can heyour some fordin fella shoutin' at hur an' hur givin' out murdur. Den all of a sudden de back of de truck slams shut an' I can't see a fukin' ting. De engine starts an' der's a loud beepin' comin' from de truck. Mudder of Jaysus, it's bleedin' reversin' out!

I start bangin' on de back door. 'Hello, hello? Der's someone in here! Tiffo? Someone get me out of here, I'm fukin' clostrafobik!'

De truck moves an' sends me flyin' on me

arse, an' den we're drivin' off to fuk knows where.

> ✉ HUN: you tik fukin bitch. im
> trapped in dis fukin truk n
> i kant get out. u find out
> off vlad wear dis ting is
> fukin goin n come n get me.
> your fukin dead when I get me
> hands on u. txt me back str8
> awey!!!! ♡
> ✉ TIFFO: i didnt no what was
> happenin vlad startd givin
> me grief 4 not returnin his
> kalls n next of all dey closd
> de truk n dey drove off he
> said de next delivery is 4
> dundawk?? X

Where de fuk is Dundawk? I sweyour if dis truck leaves me in de middle of nowhere I will fukin' murder Tiffo. I ring Whitto to try an' find out where de fuk I'm headed an' she picks up after three rings.

'Hun, I'm busy at majorettes practice wit Jazzo, wats de story?'

'Where's Dundawk?'

'Wha'? Why are ye askin' me dat?'

'Just tell me will ye! Where is it?'

'Are you doin' wan of dem word games on your phone again?'

'Yeah, dat's *exactly* what I'm doin'.'

'What's dat noise in de background? Are you in a car? What time are you comin' to de competition?'

'Whitto, for fuk's sake, *where is it*!?'

'It's in County Louth, somewhere out near Blanch, I tink. It's where de Corrs are from. Ye know yer wan dat used to be a judge on *De Voice*? Shardin Corr, dat's it.'

Next of all de truck comes to a stop an' I'm trun over sideways. An' I'm tinkin', fuk, we must be in Dundawk already.

'I'll ring ye back!' I say an' hang up.

I heyour yer man gettin' out of de front an' I start pushin' on de back door. Not a budge. I start kickin' an punchin' it an' roarin' at de top of me voice. Der's a click an' a clank outside an' de door opens. De driver fella looks in wit a big confused head on him. I grab de nearest dress to me an' take a runnin' jump out tru de door.

'What de fuk!' yer man screams as he goes flyin' backwards onto de ground.

'Verdy sorry 'bout dat mister!' I shout an' I start runnin' like it's last orders in de Hill an' I'm at de udder end of de village gaspin'.

I turn de corner an' leg it across de road an' into a Spar. I'm in a fukin' heap. I get up to de counter, pantin' an gaspin', an' ask yer man behind de counter, 'Is dis Dundawk?'

'What? You're in Coolock, love.'

'Wha'?'

Yer man is lookin' at me standin' der wit de Communion dress under me arm an' de big red face on me.

I buy a bottle of Lucozade an' go back outside to ring Tiffo.

'Hun where are ya?' she asks in a panic.

'I'm in fukin' Coolock, not fukin' Dundawk! Yer man stopped an' opened de door so I legged it.'

'Hun, you were only in de truck for twenty minutes, yer not far from home. Get a taxi back, righ'? I'll call ye later.'

I can hear a fella's voice in de background an' den she hangs up. De fukin' bitch is still der wit Vlad. Probably givin' him hand shandies out de back of Aldi. I sweyour to Jaysus.

I'm only just back at de gaff when me ma starts ringin' me.

'Where are ye? We're at the majorettes competition and Jasmine is comin' on soon. Are you nearly here?'

Fuk! I forgot all about it. 'I'm on me way, Ma, relax wud ye!' I say, an' I hang up.

I decide to hide de dress in de top press in de kitchen so I can surprise me princess wit it before she goes to school on Monday mornin'. It's only masso – pearly buttons an' a lace trim an' crystals an' all. I can't wait to see de look on Ri Ri's face!

I get down to de parish hall an' de place is jammers. Full of kids in der sparkly outfits, swingin' der batons around an' practisin' in de mirrors in de hallway. I get into de main hall an' see Whitto, me angles an' me ma wavin' at me from across de hall.

I go over to dem an' me ma starts passin' comment de minute I sit down, lookin' me up down an' givin' me filthies.

'Where were you?' she says.

'It's none of yer business,' I say, 'I had some verdy important tings to look after dis mornin'.'

De MC comes out onto de floor an' announces dat de next group up are de Fingerless Florettes. We all start roarin' out of us, jumpin' up in de seats an' cheerin' dem on. 'G'wan de Jazzo!' 'G'wan de Florettes!' De place is buzzin' an' de atmosphere is only fukin' deadly.

De music starts an' de girls start marchin' out. Verdy good choice of music. Britney's new wan.

De girls start dancin' an' goin' tru der routine an' den Jazzo de devil child comes out struttin' hur stuff at de frunt, shakin' hur arse all over de place. She's a cocky little shit, but in all fairness to hur she's de best out of de lot of dem.

She fukin' kills it! Trunnin' dat baton up in de air, cartwheelin' across de floor to catch it an' swingin' hur hips all over de place wit hur army of Florettes behind hur. De routine finishes an' everyone on our side of de hall is goin' mad. Gettin' up, standin' on de chairs, stampin' der feet in de stands. De udder side of de hall is full of fukin' tiks from de Tallaght Tannettes all sittin' der wit der arms crossed lookin' like someone just pissed in der cornflakes. Next of all one of dem stands up an' starts booin'.

'Did ye see dat kunt over der?' Whitto says to me.

'Dey're jello, dat's all!' I say. 'Don't mind 'em.'

Den me ma stands up. 'You! You over there, have some respect! Sit down!' she says wavin' hur finger at de skankbag.

Yer wan starts shoutin' back. 'Shurrup an' sit down ye oul geebag!'

Excuse me, only I'm allowed to call me ma a geebag! I get up off me seat an' me ma grabs me. 'Sit down! Don't you start makin' a show of me here!'

'Are you for fukin' real, Ma? Did you hear what she just called you?'

'Water off an old duck's back, Hun, now just sit down and relax!'

'Eh no, I'm sorry, Ma, Hun's right,' Whitto says. 'I'm not lettin' hur away wit sayin' dat about ye!'

'The two of you sit down right now!'

I climb over de seats in front of me an' march over to de cheeky kunt who's waitin' for me on de udder side.

She's standin' der wit hur hands on hur hips, an' she's real common lookin'. Hur top is bet onto hur, an' she's either pregnant or she's after swallyin' twenty buckets of KFC. Big fukin' cold sore on de side of hur face an' blue eyeshadow dat reaches halfway up hur forehead, which is so fukin' big it's a bleedin' fivehead.

'What de fuk did you call me ma?' I say to hur.

'I called hur a geebag,' she says, 'an' it's not off de fukin' stones ye licked it, ye skanky poxbottle basturd of a hooer master!'

'Dat's rich comin' from someone who has a bleedin' mickey wart on de side of hur face,' I say.

De kunt fukin' spits at me, an' dat's de last straw.

'Right, ye want a scrap?' I say rollin' up me sleeves. 'You an' me, outside, now!'

I grab hur by de hair an' drag hur outside wit half de nosey basturds in de hall follyin' us. Yer wan is screamin' out of hur an' swingin' at me an' de basturd gets me right in de eye. I knee hur as hard as I can in de gee an' she starts howlin'.

'Ye big fat basturd ye! Me fukin' fanny!'

'Dat'll teach ye to call me ma a geebag!' I roar, an' she grabs me by de ears an' starts reefin' de head off me. Der's a circle of people around us at dis stage an' de udder tiks from Tallaght are cheerin' hur on. I sweyour, it's like bein' back in primary school!

De MC comes runnin' over an' pulls us apart, an' den me ma grabs a hold of me.

'I am so sickened by your behaviour!' she starts. 'The apple doesn't fall far from the tree, does it? Fist fightin' in public, just like yer old man!'

'Are you for serdious, Ma? I was defendin' you! Yer such an ungrateful geebag!'

Me ma grabs me by de arm. 'You need to go home right now and clean yerself up. Rihanna and Tyrone will be stayin' with me tonight. I can't imagine what they must be thinkin' right now after seeing your disgraceful behaviour. Now go on, before you make any more of a show of me and yourself!'

'Ma, you are a fukin' arsehole. Unbelievable!'

I walk out tru de gates an' dat fat fuk from Tallaght stands at de door roarin' abuse after me.

'If I ever see ye again I sweyour to Jaysus I'll streel outta ye, ye kunt!'

I give hur de finger an' laugh. 'See you, ye ugly pox-face basturd? De Karma Chameeelion is gonna come for ye verdy soon ... you just WEIGHT AN' SEA!'

Faycebuk Status Update

Hun y does shite alweys happen 2 me. furst ov all de kids in de skool giv me prince n princess de kreepy krawlies n den im kidnapped in a bleedin truk. i must hav heyour luk at me im a fukin dope walk all ovur me written on me fayce ♡ ♡ xxx

---

Like – Comment – Share　　👍2　　💬10

Tiffo hun im sordy xxxxxxx

Hun dnt fukin talk 2 me u ♡

Tiffo ah hun yer gonna sea de funny side ov it next weak ha ha xxxxxxx

Hun ye in de lettin' on days ye fukin DOPE! ♡

Tiffo luv ye hun, ill call ye 2mordo xxxxxxxxxxx

Hun ♡ n de majorettez kan ask me slyce

Harley jaysus hun hope ur ok. lemme no if u need anythin x

Hun tnx babes. i need a nite in de george ♡

Harley ha ha dat kan b arranged, yer gas! X

Hun ♡

ME LI'L PRINCESS

After de competition me ma brings me angles back to hur gaff, an' later dat night she rings me givin' out stink. She starts goin' off on one, tellin' me what a bad mudder I am, sayin' I'm just like me da an' she doesn't know what she ever did to deserve me. Den she tells me dat she made Ri Ri an' Ty Ty a stew for der dinner, an' dey wudn't eat it.

'That's all your fault!' she says. 'You have a terrible diet and ye feed those kids nothing but junk. They don't know what a vegetable looks like!'

'It's not my fault ye make manky dinners,' I say, 'you've been makin' de dinner for long enough, you shud be able to make someting nice at dis stage! All you ever make is ascustin' stews an' coddles. Da hated dem as well.'

'Hun, you wouldn't know what a balanced meal was if it hit ye in the face!'

'D'ya know what, Ma? It's no wonder Da left you, de moanin' an' whingin' ye do be doin'!'

'I'll drop Rihanna and Tyrone back to your house tomorrow. I am done talkin' with you!'

An' den she hangs up on me, de basturd.

Wit me angles in der nanny's house, Saturday night an' Sunday mornin' are all about me-time. I have a few WKDs, make a luvly fry for meself an' watch de *Hollyoaks* omnibus. Me ma drops me angles back around four o'clock an' she won't even come into de gaff. Suits me, she's not welcome in anyways.

Me angles come inside an' de first ting dey do is start moanin' about how hungry dey are. Ri Ri says dat de dinner der Nanny made dem was ascustin' wit deez green tings in it, an' den she tried to make dem eat porridge dis mornin' when all dey wanted was an oul sausie an' a bit of batch. Me poor angles have been goin' tru de wars de past couple of days!

'Ma, dey were all talkin' about you after you left de majorettes competition yesterday,' Ri Ri says.

'An' wha' were dey sayin' me li'l princess of power?'

'Dey said you were rough as nails. Wha' does dat mean?'

'I'll tell ye when yer older, chicken.'

'Aunty Whitto is real mad at ye. Der was killin's after ye left. Jazzo was asqualified.'

'Are you serdious? For wha'?'

Ty Ty goes into de sittin' room to watch telly, so I bring Ri Ri into de kitchen an' pour hur a glass of red lemo. 'Now, tell me wha' happened after I left.'

'Ah Ma, ye wudn't believe it!'

After I had left dat wan from Tallaght went on de warpath, sayin' she was assaulted an' dat she was callin' de police. Der was a break before de winner of de competition was announced an' all de Florettes were gettin' grief off de Tannettes in de hallway. Turned out yer wan's daughter was de lead performer in de Tannettes an' she had killin's wit Jazzo. De two of dem were roarin' abuse at each udder an den it was war between de two teams. Dey were hittin' each udder wit der batons, reefin' de hairpieces off each udder, an' all de mudders were eggin' dem on an' cheerin'. Den de announcement was made – de Florettes an' de Tannettes had both been asqualified.

'Everyone was goin' mad. Aunty Whitto nearly had an eppo,' she says. 'It was like de apokolips!'

'G'wan,' I say, givin' hur a pack of Burger Bites, 'what happened after dat?'

Ri Ri tells me dat der was loads of roarin' an' shoutin' in de hall, wit abuse flyin' from one side to de udder. Den after a few minutes one of de judges came out onto de floor an' said dat because of de behaviour durin' de competition, an' because de two teams had killin's durin' de interval dey were both bein' asqualified.

'De fukin' Rialto Twirlers won first place!' Ri Ri says. 'Dey were shite!'

After dat it was chaos in de hall apparently, an' me ma grabbed me angles an' Jazzo an' legged it home wit dem. Whitto stayed behind to appeal to de judges, sayin' dat it was my fault for startin' de whole fukin' ting an' de Florettes wud have won first place if it wasn't for me. I sweyour, fukin' drama llamas, de lot of dem.

'An' yer Aunty Whitto is mad at me?'

'Ah Ma, she's bullin' for ye!'

Well fuk hur. Dis is de tanks I get for standin' up for dem? I'm always in de wrong. It's always my fault. Even me only sister is a user an' abuser at de end of de day. She's just as bad as de rest of dem, hur an' hur basturd devil child.

'Ma, can we get a curdy? I'm starvin'. I cudn't eat dose ascustin' tings Nanny made for us.'

'G'wan den, get de menu out of de press.'

Later, wit me angles fed an' watered, we're havin' cuddles on de couch an' watchin' *Britain's Got Talent* when I tell Ri Ri dat I have a surprise for hur before she goes to school in de mornin'.

She looks up at me 'A surprise? Wha'? What is it, Ma?'

'I can't tell ye, it's a surprise!'

'Ah Maaaa, tell me now!'

'Sorry, chicken, yer just gonna have to weight an' sea!'

De next mornin' I send Whitto a text.

✉ HUN: r u pissed off wit me? ♡
✉ WHITTO: as a matter of fakt ye
  i am xxxx
✉ HUN: ye well fuk ye ♡
✉ WHITTO: fuk u xxxx

Who de actual fuk does she tink she is? I get me housecoat on, go down de stairs an' take de Communion dress out of de top press in de kitchen. I lay it out on de table an' I can heyour me angles movin' around upstairs.

'Do yiz want Pop Tarts or Frosties for yizzer breakfast?' I roar up to dem.

Ri Ri comes leggin' it down de stairs two at a time. 'I want me surprise for me brekkie, Ma, will ye tell me what it is now?'

I bring hur into de kitchen. She takes one look at de dress an' hur jaw drops.

'Ah Ma, are ye for serdious? Is dat me dress for de Communion?'

I nod an' she truns hur arms around me an' squeezes me so hard I tink me eyes are gonna pop out of me head.

'It's gorgo! Tanks Ma!'

'Yer welcome me princess. Don't get too excited now, yer pull-ups aren't on ye yet.'

She takes de dress out of de plastic an' legs it upstairs to try it on. Next of all Ty Ty comes thumpin' down de stairs in his underwear.

'Ma, dat dress is tiny on hur,' he says. I slap him across de head.

'Don't be sayin' tings like dat, yer sister will tink she's fat.'

'Eh, she is fat Ma.'

I grab him by de arm. 'Say dat again an' I'll break yer face, d'ye heyour me?'

'Yeah, whatever Ma! Gerroff me!' he shrugs his shoulders, walks into de kitchen an' goes straight for de Pop Tarts. De pig doesn't even stick dem in de toaster, just stuffs three of dem in his gob. De li'l squealer.

Me princess comes downstairs in de dress an' de ting is fukin' bet onto hur. It's like a bleedin' mini skirt, an' de top of it is squeezin' me li'l chubmeister so much she looks like she has a big pair of diddies on hur.

'Ma, don't I look masso?' she says, an' she gives me a twirl. De ting looks like it's fit to fukin' burst any minute.

'I'll have to get it altered Ri Ri. Ye can't wear it like dat.'

'Ah Ma, why? I luv it!'

She poses in front of de mirror in de hall an' starts takin' selfies wit hur phone.

'I can't wait to show everyone in school today!'

'Eh, maybe ye shud leave it as a surprise, Ri Ri ...'

'No way! I can't wait to see der faces. Ye wudn't believe de state of some of de dresses dey've been showin' me, dey're ascustin'! Dey'll be super jello!'

Mudder of Jaysus.

Once me angles are gone I start gettin' meself bewtified for me trip to de school. I'm gonna have murder wit dat teacher. I don't know what me taxes are supposed to be payin' for, but dey're obviously not payin' for a clean school if me li'l princess is comin' home wit creepy crawlies in hur hair! I shud fukin' sue de kunts.

When I arrive at de school Speccy is sittin' behind de glass, lookin' like a snotty prick as per usual.

'I have me appointment wit Miss Murphy.'

'Oh that's right, if you'll just come with me please.'

She takes me down de hallway an' into some pokey li'l room wit a table an' two chairs. It looks like one of dem rooms where dey give you de turd agree.

'Miss Murphy will be with you shortly, please have a seat. Oh, and did you think about the sports day and where you'd be best suited?'

Fuk de sports day – I have enough on me plate without havin' to deal wit dat!

'Eh, well I'm not sure I'm free dat day after all come to tink of it!'

'We're really very short on volunteers. I'm sure you'll find a few hours to spare.'

She walks out an' closes de door behind hur. Snobby bitch.

I'm left sittin' der for a few minutes an' den I hear dis clip-clop clip-clop comin' down de hallway. Has Miss Murphy turned into a fukin' horse?

De door opens an' she skips into de room. She's one of dem really annoyin' happy-smiley fukers. Always wearin' bright colours, always in fancy shoes. I'd say she must be married to some fella who makes a ton of money 'cos der's no way she's dressin' hurself like dat bein' a teacher. Most of de teachers in dis school are in a bleedin' hoop!

Hur hair now, in fairness, is luvly.

'Where do you get your hair done, luv?' I say to hur as she shakes me hand.

'Oh!' she starts gigglin' like mad. 'You know, just one of the um, one of the salons in Dundrum.'

'It's verdy nice now, I have to say. I must get de number from ye.'

'Oh yes, of course! Now um, I know you wanted to speak with me about something in particular, but um, there is a matter that I would also like to bring up. So I will let you go first with your little bit, okay?'

Dis one is always ahemin' out of hur an' clearin' hur throat every time she speaks. I sweyour, it sounds like she still has a bit of dinner stuck down hur throat from de night before an' she can't cough it back up.

'Well, me princess came home wit durty creepy crawlies in hur hair de udder day. It was ascustin', an' de drama an' upset caused by de whole ting was disgraceful. I want to make an official complaint!'

I start tellin' hur about de cost of de shampoo an' how de school shud be payin' for it since it's der fault. I tell hur about de smell of de shampoo an' how it made all of us dry retch an' stung de eyes off me li'l princess an' she was cryin' for hours afterwards.

'So if ye don't mind me askin', what exactly are yiz doin' to make sure dis doesn't happen again?'

'Well, now,' she says, clearin' hur throat again, 'to be perfectly fair, this isn't our fault. This is something that, as we pointed out in the letter Rihanna gave you, is very normal for this age group and that happens in every primary school.'

'Has der been any udder incidents wit durty children in de school? Are der any more creepy crawlies goin' around dat I shud be worried about?'

'It's really not that the children are dirty. Lice will take a hop, skip and a jump from one clean washed head of hair to another. Since we sent the notes home it does however appear that everyone has used the shampoo as instructed and there have been no more cases of lice reported in the last three days. So, we're all "good in the hood".'

Yer wan starts clearin' hur throat again, an'

I sweyour it's startin' to serdiously get on me nerves. She opens up hur handbag an' pulls out a phone.

'Dat's funny, me princess has de exact same phone!' I say.

'Well, actually, this is Rihanna's phone. It was confiscated from her this morning.'

Miss Murphy says dat der was killin's between Ri Ri an' Jermaine Ward when she went into de class dis mornin'. Me li'l princess was showin' everyone de picture she took of herself dis mornin' in hur new Communion dress. Jermaine said it made hur look like an Oompa-Loompa an' dey started reefin' out of each udder an' Miss Murphy had to pull dem apart.

'I have intervened with Jermaine and Rihanna in the past. They seem to be "frenemies" as the kids say these days!'

'Jermaine Ward is a little knackbag. I hope she was sent to de principal.'

Yer wan just gawks at me an' clears hur throat again. I sweyour to Christ.

'After I had given them both a time-out in the bold corner, I had a look at the picture myself. I have to be perfectly honest with you – that dress is wholly unsuitable for a Communion.'

'It's a fukin' Communion dress, isn't it?'

She starts describin' de dress like me princess was a Benburb Street sluh givin' hand shandies for yokes.

'I have a feeling that the dress is simply too small for her, but in any case, the end result is that it's far too short and much too tight and exposes an unacceptable amount of skin. You simply cannot dress your child in that manner. It's just not appropriate.'

I stand up an' swipe all hur books an' pens off de table wit de back of me hand.

Miss Murphy jumps up off hur chair wit hur mouth hangin' open. 'What on earth do you think you are doing?'

'You can't talk about my daughter like dat! I'm not havin' it!'

She kneels down an' starts pickin' hur tings up off de floor, rantin' about how she thought I was a reasonable person an' she never expected behaviour like dis. Den she stands up, clearin' hur throat like mad, an' asks me to leave.

'Oh I'm leavin', don't you worry! Now gimme dat phone!'

I grab de phone out of hur hand an' tell hur dat under no circumstances is she to say dat my child is too big for hur dress ever again. She says dat she's ascusted an' dumbfounded. What de fuk does dat even mean?

I storm out of de room an' on me way out de door I walk past Speccy.

'You need to get new teachers for dis school,' I say, 'my taxes are payin' for tiks!'

'I'll have you know that our teachers all work extremely hard and the standard of teaching in this school is very high,' de snobby bitch says to me.

'Yeah, well I say all your teachers came in on de tik train.'

'The what?'

'De TIK TRAIN! Choo choo, tikko!'

I storm out tru de front gates an' head to de Hill. I need a fukin' drink after dat!

I walk into de Hill an' Robby waves me over from behind de counter. 'Jaysus, Hun, yer earlier than usual today aren't ye?'

'Gimme two WKDs, a pint glass an' a packidge of dry roasted. I'm havin' a verdy bad day so far, Robby.'

'Comin' right up, Hun!'

I tell him what happened in de school an' he tells me dat he knows all about it. His Shaneequa was in dat school before she went to secondary, he says, an' de teachers were stuck-up kunts back den too.

I take a sup of me WKD an' notice a sign on de bar.

Got a Special Occasion Coming Up?

FUNCTION ROOM AVAILABLE FOR HIRE UPSTAIRS

21st, Engagement Party, 40th Birthday, Work Event etc.

Food Available at Discounted Rates

Enquire With Bar Manager

– Special rates for regulars –

'Heyour, Robby, what's de story wit de function room?'

I tell him dat it's Ri Ri's Communion in a couple of weeks an' ask if it's available. He grabs his bookin' folder from behind de counter an' flips tru de pages.

'Yeah, Hun, it looks free alrigh', but to be honest we don't really have Communions an' that up there, d'ye know what I mean?'

'No, I don't know what ye mean. What's de problem?'

He tells me dat de manager doesn't like havin' kids up in de function room an' dey prefer 'adult only' events.

'We had an 18th up there a while back,' he says, 'an' they were all chewin' their faces, millin' bottles at each udder an' causin' trouble. They were all on yokes an' it turned out most of them were underage as well. It was a fuckin' disaster.'

'Children don't drink Robby, we'll be drinkin' – de adults. An' in fairness, we keep dis pub in fukin' bizness. Ye don't have any problem wit me angles sittin' here wit me doin' der homework on a Friday after school now, do ye?'

'Ah, c'mon Hun, that's different. Listen, let me check the diary in the back office for the staff holliers. I know the manager is off to Tenerife in a couple weeks. If he's off then it means I'm in charge while he's away, and I'll see what I can do.'

'Ah tanks, Robby, yer sound,' I say, an' he goes in de back.

De front door opens an' dis fella comes in carryin' loads of equipment. He's a li'l lash an' he looks kinda familiar. He wedges de door open wit one of de boxes an' carries in anudder load of stuff. He walks up to de bar, looks around an' says, 'Did ye see Robby anywhere?'

'He's just gone in de back der, he'll be out in a sec. C'mere to me, you look verdy familiar. Do I know ye?'

'I was just tinkin' I recognised yer face!' yer man says, lookin' me up an' down. 'Where do I know ye from?'

Den I have an atiffany – it's Mr Motorboat!

'It's Dave, isn't it? New Years Eve in De Castle two years ago, remember? You were blowin' rasperries on me diddies all night!'

He looks down at me tits, den looks back up at me wit a big grin on his face.

'Jaysus Hun, I didn't really recognise yer face but I'll never forget those baps! How have ye been?'

'Ah grand, ye know yerself! What brings ye to de Hill in anyways?'

'I'm DJ'in' for a 21st here tonight so I'm just in settin' up de equipment.' He looks me over again an gives a nervous li'l laugh. 'Jaysus, I can't get over dis! Yer tits are even bigger now dan dey used to be!'

I stick me diddies out an' give dem a shake. 'Dey're just waitin' for a good motorboatin', luv!'

Robby comes back out from behind de bar, folder in his hand.

'Yer in luck, Hun, the bastard's away all that week! I'll go ahead an' book ye in now.'

'Ah fukin' nice wan, Robby, I knew ye wud look after yer number one customer!'

Robby sees Dave an' hands him de key to de function room. 'Top of the stairs, bud,' he says, an' goes off to serve someone at de bar.

'Here, I'll come up wit ye,' I say. 'I need to have a look at de room in anyways, start plannin' me decorations.'

Dave lifts up some of de equipment an' glances at me. It looks verdy heavy.

'Sorry luv, I can't carry anyting for ye. I have a verdy sore back,' I say.

We walk up de stairs an' Dave unlocks de door. De room smells of Guinness farts an' cigarette smoke. De floor is all sticky, probably from fukin' jip. Is dis some sort of bleedin' ridin' den or wha'? If I'm goin' to have me princess's Communion party here dey better clean it up, or I'll have to come in de night before an' fukin' disinfect de place.

'Dey must never clean dis fukin' place!'

'Yeah, it's not the best is it?' Dave says, lookin' around. 'Let's crack open a window, let a bit of fresh air in.'

He puts down his equipment an' goes over to de window, bendin' down to undo de lock on de bottom. He has a luvly arse on him.

'Ye know, I happen to need a DJ for me daughter's Communion.'

'Are ye havin' it here, Hun?'

'Yeah, I am. Dat's what Robby was bookin' me in for.'

He tells me dat he doesn't usually do Communions an' dat his day rates are much higher 'cos he has to take time off from his day job. He says he'd have to check wit his boss an' get back to me an' he might not even be available dat day, an I'm like, fuk dat! I don't have all bleedin' year.

'Well, I have a job dat might just change yer mind, ye li'l ride. C'mere to me!'

He stands der like a deer in headlights. I walk over to him real serductively, wiggle me diddies in his face an' grab his crotch.

'Grand hefty mickey on ye der. Jaysus, yer like a donkey!'

'Fuckin' hell, Hun, what are ye doin'? Robby might come up!'

'Ah fuk him!'

I go to close de door, an' when I walk back over me li'l Davey boy is standin' to attention in his jeans. I open up his fly an' stick me hands right in, an' he jumps likes I'm after givin' him a bleedin' electric shock.

'Jaysus Hun, yer hands are freezin'!'

'Dey're gonna warm up in a minute, don't you worry!'

It literally was a fukin' minute, too. I only had to give his mickey a couple of squeezes an' de volcano erupted.

He zips himself up an' starts apologisin' an' sayin' he gets like dat when he's nervous.

'Yer just – yer very intimidatin'!' he stammers.

'I'm wha'?'

'Seriously, ye are. I was off me face at that New Year's Party, I'm not usually like that. Fuckin' hell, I can't believe we just did that. In here of all fuckin' places!'

'So, are ye gonna do Ri Ri's Communion party or wha'?' I say.

'Ah I dunno, Hun. Like I said, I'd have to talk to me boss an' try get time off …'

Dis fuker is startin' to piss me off. I give him me verdy best smile an' tell him I understand.

'I have to warn ye, tho, word spreads verdy quickly around de village, Davey boy. Imagine if people found out der DJ was gettin' hand shandies in de function room? Dey wudn't be verdy happy wit dat!'

'Hun, are you blackmailin' me?'

'No luv, not at all, I'm just tellin' ye de way people are around here. Dey're verdy pass-remarkibel.'

'Are you havin' a fuckin' laugh?'

'I'm dead serdious.'

In de end he sees reason an' sticks me bookin' in his diary. De poor chicken is fukin' terrified of me. On de way out I stop at de bar. 'We opened de window upstairs, Robby,' I say. 'De smell of durt up der is unnatural!'

'Thanks Hun. I hope they're not saying that about you after Rihanna's Communion party!'

'Fuk 'em. Ye know what I say – me haters are me motivaters!'

Faycebuk Status Update

Hun ye kant beat a gud oul hand shandy wit a lil ride ov a dj in yer local ha ha ♡ ♡ xxx

Like – Comment – Share   👍 3   💬 9

Whitto wat de fuk r u talkin bowt? xx

Hun ah dat wud b tellin ♡

Tiffo ye durty geebag kant believe ye did dat wit yer man lololololol xxxxxxxxx

Whitto wat did she do? xx

Hun ill tell ye wen yer older ♡

Harley hun ur a fukin durtburd LUV it, yer like dat monika looinski wan x

Hun who de fuk iz dat ♡

Harley anuddur durty bitch x

Hun fuk off ha ha ♡

ME LI'L PRINCE

Easter is a load of shite. It gives me de biggest pain in me hoop each year. De only good ting about it is de Easter eggs an' dey get smaller every year – just like Prik Feechurs an' his mini mickey. Me ma started takin' me angles to de Easter egg hunt in town when dey were small an' now I have to take dem every bleedin' year! Me ma is a dope. Harley says she sets a precedent, whatever de fuk dat means. Me angles get up on Easter Sunday an' I have a load of sausies in de pan for dem as a special treat, wit batch loaf an' loads of butter. Der's nothin' like it!

'Ma, when are we goin' in to de Easter egg hunt?' me princess asks, stuffin' half a slice of batch into hur gob.

'Close yer mouth when yer eatin', Ri Ri, yer gettin' de crumbs all over de table!'

'Ma, serdiously, don't change de subject, ye do dis every year!'

'I tink we'll give it a miss dis year, yiz are gettin' too old for dat shite. Why don't we just stay at home an' watch de telly instead, an' yiz can eat de eggs yer nanny got yiz. I'm not in de humour of goin' near town. Ty Ty doesn't care anyway, do ye me li'l prince?'

Tyrone looks at me. 'Ma, last week you promised dat we cud go an' den we cud get Eddie Rocket's after!'

Dey do be askin' me questions when I'm locked, de clever little basturds. As per usual I give in. I can't say no to me li'l angles. We stand at de bus stop for forty bleedin' minutes before de bus finally arrives.

'Yiz take yer time, don't yiz!' I say to de driver.

'It's Easter Sunday, love. We're on skeleton staff. What d'ye expect, a Garda escort into town?'

Cheeky fuker.

De bus takes for ages to get to de Garden of Remembrance. De hunt has already started but der's still a queue to sign up, an' der's fukin' fordiners everywhere. De fuk if I'm waitin' all day for dis. I tell Ri Ri an' Ty Ty to wait an' start squeezin' me way up tru de queue.

'You know, a "pardon me" wouldn't go amiss, would it?' dis voice says from behind me.

I turn around an' der's dis mahoosive fat basturd Merican starin' at me.

'Eh, 'scuze me?'

'Ma'am, you pushed right by me without so much as a beg-your-pardon. That's awfully rude of you. My goodness!'

'Listen heyour Free Willy, why don't you fuk off back to Merica an' leave us alone? De state of ye!'

He just gawks at me wit his gob open. I hope he's not waitin' for me to start trunnin' burgers in his fat face. He turns to de lady beside him.

'Marcie, did you hear what this young lady just said to me?'

I don't have time for dis shite. I push further up in de queue an' leave de Mericans standin' der wit der gobs open. Dopes! I call me angles over an' dey join me in de queue.

'Ma, de size of dem!' Ri Ri says, eyeballin' de fat basturds behind us.

'I know, Ri Ri. Dey look like dey're after eatin' everyone's bleedin' Easter eggs.'

We finally get to de front of de queue an' I fill out de registration form. Yer wan gives me a big dopey grin an' says, 'We're about half an hour in already, but there's still plenty of time to find all those yummy eggs!'

'Yeah, yeah, verdy good, see ye after,' I say. I don't have time for deez snotty-nosed tiks.

'Don't forget your first clue!' she says, an' she hands me an envelope. Me angles gather round me as I open it.

'Ma, what does de first clue say? Show us!'

We're waiting for you to come and play –
Go to where the little people are on display!

'De little people are on display?' I shake me head. What de fuk does dat mean?

'Ma, I want me Easter eggs! Figure it out will ye? Hurry up!' Ri Ri starts shoutin'.

'Give fukin' over!' I roar at hur. 'I can't tink wit all yer racket!' Me li'l Prince is standin' real still an' starin' at de ground, his eyes twitchin'. Den he looks up at us an' says, 'It's de Leprechaun Museum!'

De fukin' Leprechaun Museum – where in de fuk is dat? Tyrone starts walkin' ahead of us. 'We went wit de school last month, I know where it is!'

We get down to de museum an' it's full of bratty li'l basturd children all runnin' around reefin' eggs from every corner of de buildin'. Mudder of Jaysus, get me out of heyour!

Next ting I know Ri Ri is scrappin' wit some boy over dis cheapo fukin' Easter egg, de kind ye get in in de 2 euro shop.

'Heyour let go, dat's mine!'

'It is not! I found it and you tried to take it, that's not fair! I'm telling my mummy on you!'

I run over to de two of dem. 'What's goin' on here?'

'Ma, he won't gimme me egg back!'

'Mummy! Mummy!' de posho li'l basturd starts roarin'.

Next of all dis yoke comes runnin' over, hur high-heels clip-cloppin' on de tiles like she's a bleedin show pony. She's dressed up to de nines wit hur skinny jeans an' leather jacket. She stands der an' looks me up an' down wit hur hands on hur hips.

'What's wrong, Setanta?' she says wit a big pouty face on hur.

'Mummy, I found the egg behind that sculpture, and this girl came up behind me and grabbed it out of my hand! That's not fair!'

She looks over at Ri Ri wit dis big fake smile on hur face, an says, 'Is that true? Did Setanta have the egg first?'

Why de fuk would someone call der child after Slanty Jaws?

'No, sorry luv, my Rihanna said she found it before Santy did.'

'It's Setanta.'

'Yeah, whatever. Listen luv, you get Santy to give dat egg back to me princess an' we'll forget all about it.'

She crouches down an' pats Santy on de head. 'Come now, Setanta, give it to the little girl. There are plenty more eggs to find!'

'But Mummy, I found it …'

'Enough,' she says, before he can finish. 'Your daddy is out in the reception area – you go wait with him and I'll follow you out in just a minute. Okay, darling?'

Santy goes runnin' out of de room an' yer wan stands up an' gets right up in me face. 'Setanta *did* find that egg before your daughter, and I am reporting this incident to the organisers.'

'Yeah, well you an' Santy can fuk off, ye posh basturd geebag!'

'That's it. I'm having words with Fidelma outside – she's a very good friend of mine. This is just not on.' She's about to leave, an' den she turns back to me an' says, 'You know, it's *your* children I feel sorry for. They don't have a hope in life having you as a role model.'

Den she clip-clops hur way outside. I turn around to me angles an' say, 'I'll buy yiz de five eggs for a tenner in Tesco each if we can go to de pub now.'

'Ye whatever, once we go to Eddie Rocket's,' Ty Ty says. 'I'm fukin' starvin.''

'I don't care, as long as we go to de Communion shop on Abbey Street,' Ri Ri says.

'After de pub, Ri Ri, righ'? I'm desperate for a drink.'

She shrugs, smashes de Easter egg in hur hand den shoves half of it in hur gob. We walk tru de reception an' show pony is der makin' hur

144

complaints to Fidelma, who looks like anudder snobby posho geebag.

'We're leavin', so shove yer egg hunt up yizzer hoops!' I say, an' I give dem de finger.

'Heyour Santy, ye can have yer bleedin' egg back!' Ri Ri shouts, an' she mills de squashed-up egg at his head.

Gerrup de yard, ye gas bitch!

We leg it up de road an' head to one of de pubs on O'Connell Street. It's bleedin' jammers an' der's a group of Spanish students sittin' at a big table wit nothin' in front of dem.

'Are yiz leavin'?'

'Qué?'

'I *said* are … yiz … leavin'?'

'We are having a drink Guinness,' one of dem says.

'Speak English proper, wud ye? Yiz aren't drinkin' anytin' an' me an me angles want to sit down, so yiz can move on!' I grab one of der bags off de table. 'Now, see yiz after!' I say, an' I trun de bag out de door.

Dey all start yackin' at each udder in fordin talk an' den dey get up an' leave.

'Now, sit down der! I'll get yiz a bottle of red

lemo an' a couple packidges of crips.'

I mooch me way up to de bar an' grab de barman's attention.

'One WKD, a bottle of red lemo wit two glasses an' three packidges of King crips. One of dem salt an' vinegar.'

I turn round an' me princess has hur head down between hur legs an' she's lookin' verdy green. I leg it over to hur.

'Ma, I don't feel verdy good ...'

Den she opens hur mouth an' heaves, an' de bleedin' egg comes back up wit bits of sausage in it. Mudder of fukin' divine Jaysus.

'Right, dat's it, we're goin' home! Gerrup de two of yiz, an' don't stand in de sick!'

'I'm not goin' anywhere!' Tyrone says all of a sudden.

'I said gerrup now, we're leavin'!'

'No Ma, fuk dat, an' fuk you an' Ri Ri as well!' he roars at de top of his voice. 'I want to stay in town an' have me red lemo an' crips an' get me five Easter eggs an' *I want me Eddie Rocket's*!'

De mad basturd picks up de empty glasses on de table an' starts millin' dem at me. Den he stands up, grabs a hold of de table an' truns it upside down.

'Ma, I'm scared!' Ri Ri says, hur mouth hangin' open. 'Dat's de worst eppo I ever seen him have!'

De bar man legs it over an' starts roarin' at us. 'Get out of this pub right now, before I call the Gardaí!' Jaysus fukin' Christ almighty, what de fuk is goin' on?

Den suddenly Ty Ty legs it out de front door.

'Tyrone, come back here, ye li'l prick!' I roar. I grab Ri Ri an' we run out after him. O' Connell street is fukin' jammers wit people an' I can't see a ting. De li'l basturd has disappeared.

> ✉ HUN: tyrone iz after havin n eppo in de pub in o Connell street n hez leggd it wer r u ♡
> ✉ WHITTO: im in town aswell wit ma n jazzo he kant b gone far xxxx
> ✉ HUN: meet me at de gpo in 10 mins ♡

We head to de GPO an' me ma, Whitto an' Jazzo are all der.

'We were in the middle of a lovely afternoon tea in the Earl,' me ma says. 'What did you do this time?'

'Don't fukin' start on me, Ma, dis isn't my fault!'

She tuts at me. 'Would you ever stop using language like that in front of the chislers? It's no wonder Tyrone ran off on ye!'

'De two of yiz stop it!' Whitto says, gettin' in between us. 'We need to split up an' try to find him. He can't be gone far. An' knowin' him he's probably sat down stuffin' his face somewhere.

Whitto an' Jazzo go off to look in Mickey Dee's, me an' Ri Ri head down to Eddie Rocket's an' me ma goes to Burger King.

We search everywhere an' der's no sign of him. I'm startin' to get serdiously worried when me ma rings me.

'I found him,' she says.

'Tanks be to Jaysus! Where was he?'

'GameStop. A security guard had a hold of him – he had three games stuffed down his trackies.'

'De li'l gicknah!' I say. 'I'll kill him!'

'Hun, go easy on him for once, will ye? He's very upset.'

When we meet back up, Ty Ty is hangin' his head like he's four years old an' been caught rapid sneakin' pink wafers from de biscuit tin. He's real quiet an' sulky. I run over an' give him a big hug an' he just stands der, lookin' at de ground.

'Ye fukin' eejit, why did ye run off like dat? I was worried sick!'

De li'l basturd doesn't say a word. Whitto pulls me to one side. 'Hun, why don't I look after Ri Ri for a li'l while so you can talk to Ty Ty?'

'Ah tanks, Whitto, nice wan.'

'C'mon girlos,' Whitto says, 'I'll bring yiz to de Communion shop on Abbey Street.'

We leave de udders an' wander off down de O'Connell Street togedder. Ty Ty is real quiet for a while, an' I'm half tinkin' to meself, what if dis mad basturd flips out again an' does anudder legger on me?

'Ma, I'm sick of dis Communion!' he says after a few minutes. 'I'm sick of Ri Ri gettin' all de attention. How come yiz never made a big deal when it was my Communion?' Den he goes all quiet again an' sticks his hands in his trackies. 'I just feel verdy left out,' he says.

'Ah now, me li'l prince – well, yer me big man now really, aren't ye? I'm verdy sorry for makin' ye feel dat way. I'll make it up to ye, I promise. Is there anyting I can do to cheer ye up?'

He tinks about it for a minute.

'Yeah ma, I want a bucket of KFC to meself an' two tubs of gravy. I'm fukin' starvin'.'

'A bucket of KFC it is, Ty Ty. Whatever ye want, me li'l prince.'

Den he gives me a proper big hug, an' we meet up wit de udders again for a quick WKD an' a red lemo. De li'l basturd gets his bucket of KFC on de way home an' sits on de settee stuffin' his mush an' playin' his Xbox an' he's as happy as a pig in shite.

I'm a single mudder, an' a verdy strong wan at dat, but even I can't be dealin' wit everyting deez li'l basturds trun at me sometimes. So de next day I go to see Ty Ty's teacher, an' he says Tyrone shud talk to de school counsellor. De li'l basturd does it an' all. He's been to see yer wan a few times – I've no idea what dey talk about but it seems to be sortin' him out. I tink it calms him down a bit – he stops kickin' de bleedin' bin all de time in anyways. I try to talk to him more often as well. Half de time he just says 'Whatever, Ma,' but I tink he likes de attention.

I never thought dat Tyrone might be missin' his da. I thought growin' lads were supposed to be smashin' tings up an' actin' like cavemen! Apparently I was wrong. When I tink about it, I was totally in bits when me own da left. Maybe I shud have paid more attention to me li'l prince.

By de week before de Communion, I'm at me wits end. Me li'l princess is costin' me a bleedin' fortune an' I can't pay for it all meself. I decide dat me only option is to try an' get me ma on side so she'll pay for some of it. What udder choice do I have?

> ✉ HUN: ma i need 2 talk 2 ye r ye home ♡
> ✉ MA: YES.I.AM.HOME.
> ✉ HUN: ill be over 2 ye in n hour. its about de Communion ♡
> ✉ MA: I.AM.GOING.TO.BINGO.HURRY. UP.

How de fuk does she write texts? De dope.

I haven't set foot inside me ma's gaff in months an' I'm fukin' dreadin' it. When I knock on hur door dat afternoon, Whitto is de one who opens it.

'What are you doin' here?' I ask hur.

'Ma thought we shud all sit down an' have a chat about de Communion togedder.'

'For fuk sake! You set dis up, didn't ye?'

'Get in will ye, she has bingo in a while.'

I go inside an' me ma is sittin' der like lady muck. De house is de exact same as it's always been – de picture of de Pope over de mantelpiece, de li'l figurines on de windowsill, de manky brown furniture. Ye tink she'd redecorate every once in a while. Der's a pot of tae on de table an' a plate of biscuits. Dat's de one good ting ye can say about dis place – der's always a cuppa on de go.

I sit down beside hur an' she pours de tae.

'Now, what did you need to talk to me about?'

I didn't want to have to say dis in front of Whitto, but she's standin' der starin' at me. What de fuk is she doin' here?

'Ma, I need a lend for de Communion.'

She rolls hur eyes an' says, 'I knew it. You always come crawlin' when you're lookin' for money.'

'Hun, me an' Ma have a plan,' Whitto says as she plonks herself down on de settee.

Dey both start talkin' about de fact dat Jazzo an' me princess are havin' der Communion on de same day, an' dat it makes sense for dem to have de party an' all togedder to save on money. Whitto goes all red in de face an den she tells me dat Jazzo's da stopped sendin' money over to hur months ago, an' dat she's fuked for de Communion.

'So it was all fukin' bullshit? De princess dress, de tiara, de bouncy castle – you an' Jazzo were rubbin' all dat stuff in our faces an' it wasn't even true?'

'No, Hun, it wasn't. I'm fukin' broke. I was morto. I didn't want to say anyting an' I hadn't de heart to tell Jazzo either. She was so exirrah, I cudn't break hur heart like dat.'

'You made it worse for yourself, Whitney,' me ma says, sippin' hur tea. 'You should have come and told me about this in the first place instead of lettin' it all go on for so long.'

An' den she turns on me. 'And *you*! You and your dodgy goin's on. It's no wonder Ri Ri is gettin' such a hard time in school! Jasmine told me about the dress you got her and how small it is. It obviously came off the back of a lorry if it doesn't fit her properly!'

Little does she fukin' know.

'I don't care what you two get up to, but me granchislers are my priority here. So I have a plan.'

I sweyour to Jaysus, she's like a little fukin' Hitler sittin' in de corner wit hur cup of tae.

'Whitney bought a dress for Jasmine in the Oxfam shop and it's far too big for her. If you swap dresses, I'll alter them to fit the girls properly,' she says.

'Eh, I haven't seen Jazzo's dress yet. For all I know it cud be mank!' I say.

'Hun, shut up! You will swap dresses and I will bleach, steam, repair, and add any embroidery that is needed. You are both to share this pink car thing …'

'Pink Hummer *limo*!' me an' Whitto say at de same time.

'Yes, yes, whatever it is. We'll use the function room to have a joint party. I'll make the finger food for it and we'll go to the euro shop for decorations and balloons and that.'

She smirks an' starts pourin' out more tae. Cool as a cucumber. I sweyour, she has dis all worked out. Once again she is dictatin' exactly what is goin' on in our lives.

Whitto is sittin' der, 'yeah yeah yeah' out of hur. Agreein' wit everyting me ma says.

'How long have you had dis planned for, Ma?' I ask.

'Hun, I have been plannin' out your life for you since you were shitin' green.'

'Dat's ascustin'.'

'Is Harley still available to come and do the hair and make-up?'

'Yeah, he is.'

'Good. That's all sorted then. Once again, I have sorted the two of yiz out!'

She starts tidyin' away de tae an' biscuits an' brings dem into de kitchen. Me an' Whitto are lookin' at each udder makin' faces, takin' de piss outta me ma. I tink we've made our peace.

'Right, I'm off to bingo,' she says, puttin' on hur coat. 'Hun, get me something in writing for the cost of the function room, disc jockey and the pink car and I will sort that out so we don't lose any of our bookings. Now move, the two of yiz! Yer mammy has a date with a barrel of balls.'

Durty oul bitch.

De next week everyting seems to be comin' along smoothly in de run up to de Communion. Me ma, as much of a head wreck as she is, has paid for everyting an' has nearly finished all de work on Ri Ri an' Jazzo's dresses. I was all calm an' collected, an' den it dawned on me. De fukin' sports day.

'Ty Ty, when is yer sports day?' I shout up to him from de livin' room.

'It's tomorrow, Ma!' he roars back. Fuk!

When I spoke to Ty Ty's teacher about his anger management issues he told me to get him involved in football or someting like dat. He started playin' hurley – ye know, de wan wit de sticks. I personally wudn't be givin' him a big wooden stick to hit people wit, but his teacher said he was gettin' on well an' it helped wit his anger an' all. I don't want to miss seein' me li'l prince play in de sports day, but I can't believe I got meself roped into helpin' out wit all dis udder shite.

De next day Speccy is der in hur fukin' shorts an' leg warmers, runnin' on de spot wit de udder kids like she's Mr bleedin' Motivator. I walk over to hur an' she sighs an' says, 'You were supposed to be here an hour ago!'

'I arrive when I'm good an' ready, tank you verdy much. Where are de udder parents?'

'It's just us and the two PE teachers. One other parent signed up but unfortunately there was a family emergency and she had to cancel.'

I look across de field an' der's millions of smelly little basturd children runnin' all over de place. I can deal wit me own flesh an' blood but I can't be fukin' dealin' wit dis shit. Speccy hands me a box an' I open it up.

'What's dis?'

'Spoons! You know, for the egg and spoon race? Please tell me you remembered the hard-boiled eggs.'

Fuk.

'Eh, yeah of course, dey're just over der in me bag.'

I turn around to Ty Ty an' whisper in his ear. 'Here's 2 euro. Leg it down to de Spar an' get a half-dozen eggs.'

'But Ma!'

'But nothin', now g'wan, an' hurry!'

Ty Ty comes back a few minutes later wit de eggs. 'Good lad,' I say, 'I'll bring ye for a Mickey Dee's after.'

Speccy starts blowin' on hur whistle an' waves me over.

'There's six students per race, here's the list of who is going when. When I call their names, they'll come up and collect an egg and a spoon from you, okay?'

She starts callin' out names, an' de li'l toerags come up to me one by one. I join Speccy at de startin' line an' one of de li'l basturds shouts, 'I didn't get an egg!'

Speccy takes de last egg out of de box an' looks at me. 'Did you only bring six?'

'Eh, yeah, it's six in a race isn't it?'

'Well, it's a good thing that these have been hard-boiled then, isn't it? Here, Jason. Catch!'

Jason holds up his hands an' she truns de egg at him. He misses it, an' it gets him right in de face.

'Ahhh, me face! Me eyes! Ye tik bitch!' he screams.

She turns round an' looks at me wit hur gob hangin' open.

'Didn't you hard-boil these last night?' she asks.

'I must have forgot,' I say. 'Verdy sorry about dat.'

'Right, it looks like we'll have to cancel the egg and spoon race. Everyone get back over against the goal posts, we're going to move straight onto the five-a-side soccer! Come on, boys, move it!' An' she starts blowin' on hur whistle.

De day fukin' drags in. Speccy is a controllin' kunt for most of it, treatin' me like hur bleedin' slave an' havin' an eppo when I sneak behind de bushes for a quick fag. De best part of de day is gettin' to see me li'l prince beatin' de absolute bejaysus out of de udder boys in de hurlin' match an cheerin' him on. By de time we get home, I'm bleedin' knackered.

I'm just sittin' down wit a mug of tae when I look out de window an' see someone hoverin' outside de gate. I leg it out de door an' der's

Jasinta from number 82 tryin' to rob me fukin' wheelie bin.

'Jasinta, what de fuk do you tink yer doin'?'

'Your Tyrone took my wheelie bin an' fuked it in de canal last week,' she says. 'Joan Fitzgerald down de road told me so!'

'Oh yeah? Where's yer proof? Get yer bleedin' hands off dat fukin' wheelie bin before I rip de head off yer shoulders, ye kunt.'

'Fair's fair, this is my wheelie bin now!'

She starts runnin' across de road wheelin' de fukin' ting in front of hur. I leg it after hur an' just as she gets to hur gate I grab hold of hur hair an' reef hur backwards. She turns around an rams de bin as hard as she can into me legs, sendin' me flyin' backwards. Den she opens up de wheelie bin an' truns it on its side.

'Mudderfuker!'

She empties de contents of de bin over me an' laughs. I'm sittin' der covered in mouldy tea bags an' take-away wrappers an' bleedin' badayta peels.

Den I hear me li'l princess's voice. 'Leave my ma alone, ye hairy-faced geebag!'

G'wan de Ri Ri! I look up an' der's me two li'l

angles lookin' like dey're fit to murder dat nosey pass-remarkibel.

Tyrone pushes de wheelie bin over, den picks up a brick an' fuks it at Jasinta. She ducks an' it goes flyin' over hur head an' smashes tru hur window.

'I'll trun you *in* de wheelie bin before I fuk it in de canal de next time!' he roars.

Jasinta crawls over to hur frunt door an' disappears inside. Hur net curtains are flappin' tru de broken window an' der's rubbish all over hur front garden.

'Ma, ye have badayta peels all over yer face,' Ri Ri says to me, pickin' a tea bag out of me hair.

'I know I do, chicken, but I also have de best angles a mudder cud ask for. Curdy an' cuddles for de both of yiz.'

'Nice wan, Ma!'

'Yeah, tanks Ma.'

De two of dem help me up off de ground an' leg it inside de gaff to get de menu.

'Anyting yiz want off dat menu tonight,' I say. 'A special treat for standin' up for yer ma!'

Faycebuk Status Update

Hun its bad enuff dealin wit yer own lil basturd children but havin 2 deal wit uddur kids dat smell ov nit shampoo nevur agen i wont get trapped like dat agen ♡ ♡ xxx

Like – Comment – Share 👍3 💬13

Tiffo ah hun how did ye get on? Xxxxxxxx

Hun fukin stupid i sweyour ♡

Whitto bit ov exercise 4 ye xx

Hun whitto serdiously fuk off ♡

Whitto im only havin a laff hun xx

Hun not in de humour. verdy sordy ♡

Harley ah hun I bet ye got yer t-shirt wet for all de dilfs dat wear der x

Tiffo ha ha Harley yer gas i bet she did n all de durty bitch xxxxxxxxx

Hun wat de fuk is a dilf ♡

Harley das id like 2 fuk x

Hun ders nun ov dem in de skool just sluh mudders wit 20 kids frum diffrint das ♡

Whitto pot n kettle hun. pot n kettle xx

Hun swivvle on it ♡

FIRST COMMUNION DAY

After weeks of killin's de big day is finally here.
I'm lyin' in me nice comfy bed as snug as a bug,
but I've been awake for hours. Me mind's racin'.
All of a sudden it sounds as though der's a herd
of baby elephants in the next room. Here we
go! Ri Ri is fukin' bouncin' around de house.
She barges into me bedroom an' jumps on de
bed.

'Ma, Ma, I'm so exirrah! When is Harley
comin' to do me make-up?'

'Happy Communion day, me li'l puddin',
I say, givin' hur a big hug an' a kiss. 'He's gonna
be here at nine. Go downstairs der an' get out all
de make-up ye want him to use, de bag is under
de sink. Jazzo is gonna be here soon.'

She legs it down de stairs an' I trun on a
housecoat an' folly hur.

Der's a knock on de door an' it's Whitto an' Jazzo. Whitto has rollers in hur hair an' she's carryin' de dresses all wrapped up in plastic.

'Where's Ma?' I ask.

'She's gonna meet us at de church, Hun,' Whitto says, 'I have all de udder bits an' bobs dat she sorted for Ri Ri in me bag.'

I'm about to shut de door when Harley appears wit a big grin on his face.

'Heyaaass!'

He skips in tru de hallway an' Ri Ri an' Jazzo start swinging out of him.

'Harley, do me first!' Jazzo says.

'No, me first, it's my gaff!' Ri Ri says, pushin' Jazzo out of de way.

'Jaysus, Hun, Rihanna looks like she just got back from Santa Ponza!' Harley says.

'I did de Santra Pay on hur last night. What do ye tink?'

'Ah Hun, she's gorgo. A bewtifel golden-brown canvas for me to work on.' He turns to me princess, 'Ri Ri, get up on dat chair der an' I'll start gettin' yer face did!'

Harley starts workin' his magic an' after he's done, Ri Ri legs it to de bathroom an' looks in de mirror. He's after givin' hur luvly rosey cheeks an' bewtiful fire engine red lips. Hur eyeshadow is three shades of pink wit loads of glitter, an' de diamond eyelashes are just to die for.

'Ma, Ma, I look like Hunny Boo Boo when she does de pageants!'

'I know, chicken, yer only masso!'

She runs back over to Harley an' hugs him. 'Tanks, Harley, yer de best!'

'Yer very welcome, chicken! Now Jasmine, jump up on dat chair and I'll start on you. Hun, you get a start on Ri Ri's hair.'

An hour later all de hair an' make-up is done an' de two li'l princesses go upstairs to get der dresses on. Whitto has dem laid out on me bed an' dey're just de picture of bewty. In fairness to me ma she got de finger out an' did a deadly job on de oul switcharoo. Ri Ri an' Jazzo are both verdy happy in anyways, dat's de important ting.

After Ri Ri gets into hur dress she looks in de mirror an' starts screamin'. 'Ma, I'm only bleedin' gorgeous!'

'I know ye are, me princess of power! Now c'mere till I get a picture of yiz on me iPhone.'

Me ma has put crystals an' silver embroidery all over de dress, an' wit de sun comin' tru de window de sparkle comin' off hur is unreal. Jazzo looks gorgo as well, an' de li'l bitch is so delighra wit hurself dat for once she's not tryin' to cause rukshunz. I look around an' Tyrone is standin' in de doorway wit a big sulky head on him.

'Doesn't yer sister an' yer cuz look de part?'

'Yeah, dey look like dopes!'

'Tyrone, if you start wit all dis shite again today I sweyour I will fukin' batter ye. Now g'wan an' put yer new clothes on an' wash yer mush. D'ye hear me?'

'Yeah Ma, whatever!' he says, an' he kicks de door an' skulks off down de landin'. De ungrateful l'il fukur has new Timberlands, masso jeans from Unique an' a luvly jumper from Superdry. He doesn't appreciate anyting I give him!

Whitto leans into me ear. 'Make sure he takes dem tablets de doctor gave him,' she whispers. 'De last ting we need is him havin' an' eppo in de church.'

'I know, don't worry. I'll crush dem up an'

trun dem in his red lemo.'

De girls run downstairs an' me an Whitto start gettin' ourselves ready for de church. I'm wearin' de dress to put all udder dresses to shame. It's pink, it's glittery, it's nearly showin' off me gee but subtle enough dat it isn't, an I've got deez masso giraffe skin heels to go wit it. No Penneys gear for me today, it's New Look all de way! Only de best for me princess's Communion! I swear de priests will be wantin' to ride me I'm such a li'l lash. I'm puttin' in me extensions when me phone starts ringin' an' I pick it up, tinkin' it must be Lemmy callin' about de Hummer.

'How'ye Lemmy, are ye on yer way out already?'

'No, Hun, it's me. I'm after gettin' out on day release for de Communion. Gimme de details so I can meet ye at de church, will ye?'

PRIK FUKIN' FEECHURS!

'Eh, verdy sorry you must have de wrong number!' I say, an' I hang up in a panic.

'Whitto, dat was fukin' Prik Feechurs on de phone, he said he's after gettin' day release an' he's comin' to de Communion!'

'Yer fukin' jokin' me!'

'I wish I was! Fuk him. Verdy sorry but he's not ruinin' me princess's big day!'

I turn off me phone an' stick it in me pocket. Next ting I can hear a car horn beepin' an' de girls start goin' mad downstairs.

'Maaaa, de pink Hummer is outside!' Ri Ri starts roarin'.

Me an' Whitto grab our stuff an' head downstairs. Harley is packin' up all de make-up.

'Harley, are ye comin' wit us?' I say.

'Eh, of course, Hun. I'd fukin' love a ride in that!'

'Get all de make-up togedder, will ye? For de touch-ups after de church.'

We all go outside an' Ri Ri an' Jazzo are jumpin' up an' down like mad tings. If dey don't fukin' calm down dey're gonna break a leg or Ri Ri is gonna end up bein' Polly fukin' Pissy Pants.

Lemmy gets out of de Hummer an' opens up de back door for us. Verdy posh.

'What kind of car is this? Yer makin' a show of the estate!' I heyour from across de road. Jasinta from number 82 is comin' over in hur housecoat for a fukin' nose as per usual.

'Fuk off, Jasinta, I'm not in de humour of ye today, right? Dis is my Ri Ri's big day an' yer not gonna spoil it!'

Next of all Tyrone comes out de door in his good clothes wit a bag of apples an' starts millin' dem at Jasinta.

'Go an' fuk off, ye geebag basturd!' He roars as he fuks de apples at hur. She shouts an' swears out of hur an' den Tyrone gets hur right in de face an' she legs it back inside whimperin'.

'Good lad, Tyrone!' I say. 'Now jump in der an' sit beside yer sister. Lemmy, put on some tunes der. Let's get dis show on de road!'

We drive off an' all de nosey pass-remarkibel neighbours are standin' in der front gardens starin' at us as we go by. De dopes wuldn't know class if it bit dem on de bollix.

We're gettin' close to de church when Ri Ri starts whimperin'. 'Ma, I need to go de toilet!'

'I sweyour to fukin' Jaysus Ri Ri, I told you to go before we left de gaff!'

I cudn't put pull-ups on hur 'cos she wanted to wear de frilly nickurs dat me ma bought hur. If she piddles hur ninnies in dat bleedin' dress

I'll fukin' streel out of hur!

'Ma, give us me red lemo,' Jazzo is sayin'. 'I'm dyin' of de thirst!'

Whitto roots around in hur bag an' pulls out a bottle.

'Heyour, mind ye don't spill dat!' she says.

Jazzo takes a sup an den hands de bottle to Ri Ri.

'Yer not havin' any of dat, Ri Ri! Ye just said yer dyin' for de toilet!' I'm just about to swipe de bottle off hur when de Hummer hits a fukin' speed bump, an' de red lemo goes gushin' all over Ri Ri's gorgeous dress. She looks up at me wit tears wellin' up in her eyes, an' den she turns to Jazzo an' gives hur an almighty thump.

'Ye did dat on purpose, ye fukin' bitch!' she screams.

'I did not! Dat was yer ma's fault, not mine!' Jazzo roars back at hur.

Harley is rootin' tru his manbag. He takes out a towel an' starts wipin' Ri Ri's dress.

'It's only a l'il drop, chicken,' I say. 'We'll dry ye off inside, you'll be grand!'

Jazzo is climbin' up onto Whitto's lap tryin' to get away from Ri Ri an' de red lemo runnin' all over de seat. Me an' Harley are tryin' to calm me princess down but she looks like she's about to have a fukin' eppo. All of a sudden de limo stops an' we're outside de church.

We all climb out as quick as we can an' I wave at Lemmy tru de front window. 'Nice wan Lemmy, see ye at two, yeah?'

We're leggin' it up to de church doors when Lemmy jumps out of de driver's seat like his arse is on fire.

'Heyour! Yiz are after spillin' somethin' back there!' he's roarin' after us. 'De seat's soaked! Der's an eighty euro soilage charge for dat, I'll have ye know!'

'Shove it up yer hoop!' I shout back, 'I'm not payin' ye another cent, ye pervert!'

Whitto is cursin' me under her breath. 'Fukin' great, der goes our ride to de Hill!' she says. 'We'll have to get a taxi!'

'Don't start on me, Whitto, yer Jazzo did dat on purpose!' I say, givin' hur filthies. 'Now yous go on inside, I'm gonna get Ri Ri dried off in de back.'

I bring Ri Ri in tru de side door an' der's a priest standin' in de hallway.

'You have to go through the main doors for the church,' he says, lookin' me up an' down. 'This is the sacristy.'

'Ah Father, I need to dry off me li'l princess. She's after drenchin' hurself in red lemo in de Hummer.'

Ri Ri is snivellin' an' drippin' red lemo all over de carpet. He stares at de two of us an' starts frownin'. Fukin' dope.

'You can use that room over there, but you need to hurry up. The service starts in ten minutes.'

'Nice wan, Father. Sound.'

I go into de side room wit Ri Ri an' look around for someting to rinse hur off wit. I find a tea towel an' start rubbin' at de red lemo stains, but dey're goin' nowhere. Me poor princess's dress is ruined.

'Ma, look,' she says, 'wha' about dat?' I turn around an' de mad bitch is pointin' at a big bottle wit a blue lid in de shape of de Virgin Mary.

'Dat's holy water, Ri Ri!' I say. 'De priest wud fukin' murder me!'

'But *Maaaa*, me dress!' she whinges, an' she starts snivellin' again.

'Alrigh', wud ye shurrup!' I grab de bottle an' pour it over de end of hur dress, an' just like magic de stains start to come out. I give hur anudder rub down wit de tea towel an' she's as good as new.

'Righ', yer sorted, now c'mon or dey'll start without ye!'

We leg it back outside an' run tru de main doors of de church. All de udder children are in der seats already. We're walkin' up de aisle lookin' for Whitto an' Jazzo when out of de corner of me eye I spot him: Prik Feechurs is sittin' in a pew wit a guard either side of him. I sweyour I almost fukin' die. How de fuk did he find out were we were?

'Ma, look, it's me da!' Hur face lights up an' she starts roarin' an' wavin' at him like a mad ting. 'Da! How'ye Da!'

'How'ye, me princess! Ye look a picture, ye really do!' He waves back at hur an' he's in fukin' handcuffs an' all. I sweyour to Jaysus.

Everyone turns around to look an' I'm fukin' morto. I spot me ma an' de udders up at de top of de church an' leg it up to dem. We squeeze in on de bench beside dem an' me ma is givin' me filthies.

'Did you tell Prik Feechurs where we were?' I whisper to hur.

'Hun, he's her father, he's blessed that he could see her make her Communion. He called me earlier sayin' you hung up on him when he rang ye this mornin', so of course I told him where the service would be. Honestly, I'm ashamed of you. Now be quiet and try to have some respect in God's house!'

Once again me ma is stickin' hur nose in my bizness. When will dis ever fukin' end? De music starts up an' de choir start singin'. Dey sound like a bunch of strangled cats. De priest walks out onto de altar an' already I'm tinkin', dis better not take too long. Dis place gives me de fukin' willies.

'Der's dat penguin Sister Immaculata up at de top,' I whisper in Whitto's ear. 'She's a right nosey bitch.'

'Hun, shurrup.'

'Fuk ye.'

A few minutes in an' I'm already dyin' wit de boredom listenin' to all de usual bollix about prayin' an' goin' to Mass on Sunday an' fukin' whatever else de priest was goin' on about.

Serdiously, Communions are about bewtiful dresses an' money an' presents an' makin' yer angles look like li'l princes an' princesses. Dey're not about all dis 'Body of Christ, He is de Lamb of de World, an' de field of God is where de lambs have der dinner an' der tea' bollix. Fukin' borin' de poor kiddies an' scarin' dem wit all der weirdo stories. Me l'il princess doesn't want to be eatin' someone's bleedin' flesh. Dat's fukin' ascustin'.

Sister Immaculata starts usherin' de children up to de altar. De udder kids are in bits – serdiously, de absolute hack of der outfits. Dey're real cheap lookin' at der's no glamour to them. De udder li'l girls don't even have any make-up on! Are der parents for real? Ri Ri an' Jazzo stand out a mile.

Sister Immaculata obviously tinks so as well 'cos she's starin' me li'l princess out of it wit hur mad beady eyes. Next ting I know she leans in an' grabs Ri Ri by de arm an' starts sayin' someting in hur ear.

'Get yer hands off my princess, ye bleedin' penguin!' I say, standin' up in de pew. Me ma tries to hold me back but I get out of me seat an' storm up to hur. She looks up at me wit an' ascusted expression on hur face.

'Are you Rihanna's mother? She should *not* be wearing eyelashes like those in the church! They're highly inappropriate!' she folds hur arms an glares at me, 'I've asked her to go to the sacristy to remove them.'

'Listen heyour, ye nosey pass-remarkibel, I'm Ri Ri's ma, an' if you lay anudder finger on hur I sweyour to Jaysus I'll break it!

Yer wan starts lookin' real nervous. Everyone in de church is starin' at us an whisperin'. Me ma has a face on hur like thunder.

'There's no need to be so aggressive,' Sister Immaculata says. 'Now, if you'd just return to your seat …'

I get right up in hur face an' lower me voice. 'I had enough of your kind when I went to school, makin' me eat black bananas an' whackin' de hands off me wit yizzer leather straps. You touch my child *one more time* an' I will end you. Do I make meself clear?'

'Perfectly,' she says, an' she gulps an' walks back up to de front.

'Good on ye, Hun!' I turn around an' der's

Tiffo wit a big grin on hur face.

'Ah nice wan, ye made it!'

'I wudn't miss dis for de world, Hun. Especially when yer ruffin' up one of dem penguins! Fukin' class!'

De ceremony finally ends, an' I turn around to me ma. De soppy bitch is gone all teary-eyed seein' Jazzo an' Ri Ri get der First Holy Communion an' she's moppin' hur face wit a hanky.

'Where's de photographer?' I ask.

She sighs. 'They aren't allowed in the church. He'll be at the Hill.'

'It's 'cos of de profiteroles, Hun,' Whitto says. 'Ye know, de wans dat do be interferin' wit de kiddies.'

'Oh righ.'

I look around an' Prik Feechurs is startin' to walk out of de church. He waves at Ri Ri an' she legs it down from de altar to give him a big hug an' a kiss. I guess me ma's right – he is hur da at de end of de day, even if he's a basturd. Deep breaths, Hun, I tink, deep breaths. He'll be gone in a few hours.

We get outside an' Ri Ri an' Jazzo are gettin'

pictures taken wit der friends. Dey're all mad jello, complimentin' dem on der hair an' make-up.

'Yer diamond eyelashes are only gorgeous!'

'I *love* yer pink lipstick.'

'My ma wudn't let me wear make-up, de bitch! It's not fair!'

Ri Ri points at Harley. 'Dat's me ma's friend Harley who did de make-up on us,' she says at de top of hur voice. 'He's a drag queen!'

'Mam, what's a drag queen?' One of de girls asks hur mudder who looks verdy confused.

Harley is standin' der grinnin' like he has a coat hanger in his mouth.

I'm takin' pictures of Tiffo an' Ri Ri on me iPhone when I get a tap on me shoulder. I turn around an' it's dis fella in a fancy uniform an' a hat. 'Are you Christina?' he says.

'Ehh …'

'The chauffeur who was with you this morning had to go home, so I'll be dropping you to the reception. I'll be waiting over here when you're ready.' He points over at a white limo parked on de corner of de street facin' de church.

179

Bingo! I don't know who Christina is an' I don't care – dis is our ride to de Hill. Ye snooze ye lose. Pity about ye. I gather everyone together an' we leave de church grounds.

'We have a replacement limo. It's not pink but it's better than nothin'.'

De girls are delighra. We all squeeze into de limo an' I tell de driver where we're goin'.

'I thought you were going to the Seafront Hotel?'

'Change of plan, luv.'

Me ma looks at me sideways. 'Hun, what happened to this pink Hummer you were gettin'?'

'We got it earlier Nanny, but we spilled red lemo in it an' he was ragin' an de driver wuldn't bring us to de Hill!'

'Ri Ri, for Jaysus sake shurrup!'

We get to de Hill an' Robby brings us upstairs. De place is only masso! Der's balloons all around de room an' a big banner on de wall dat says 'Princesses' Communion.' All de tables have party poppers an' dat luvly silver confetti stuff on dem. Robby did a brill job settin' de place up.

'How'ye, Hun, I'm gonna set up over here, alrigh'?'

I turn around an' der's Dave lookin' like a rabbit caught in headlights. De poor chicken is terrified.

'How'ye Davey Boy, sounds great! Don't worry, I won't bite.' Not yet in anyways!

He looks at me an' his face goes bright red. 'Eh, I have a playlist, ye can have a look at it there if ye want. Is there, eh, anyting ye want me to add to it?'

'Just play whatever Ri Ri an' Jazzo want to hear, alright? An' for fuk sake, stop actin' like I'm gonna hop on ye. Maybe later, wha'? Gerrup de yard!' an' I give him a smack on de arse. Luvly arse it is too.

'Eh, nice one, yeah. Okay. Grand.' An' he starts goin' tru his CDs wit a big morto face on him.

A few minutes later people start arrivin'. De place soon fills up wit me bestos, some of Ri Ri an' Jazzo's li'l friends, an' de few relatives an' neighbours I can actually stand. Jasinta from number 82 isn't invited in anyways, dat's for sure! I look for me ma an' find hur drinkin' a sherry over at de bar. 'Where's de food?'

'It's on a table over in the corner. I had it brought over this mornin'. No sign of your father yet, I see!' she says, an' she downs de rest of hur sherry in one go.

'Yeah, no thanks to you,' I say. 'You've probably been sendin' him death threats!'

I go to have a look at de food. Surprise surprise, Tyrone is at it already.

'Get away from der, we're not havin' de food yet. Yer gonna have to wait till everyone gets here!'

'But Ma, I'm starvo!'

Me ma pops up beside me. She has anudder sherry in hur hand already. 'Oh for Jaysus sake, let the child have a sandwich if he's hungry! He's a growin' lad!'

Crash, bang, wallop! De tray falls off de table an' der's egg sambos an' sausage rolls all over de ground. Tyrone just stands der like he's frozen to de spot. Robby an' de udder barman come over an' start pickin' dem up. 'D'ye want to try and salvage any of these Hun?' Robby says.

'No, trun dem in de bin, dat floor is filthy durty. Tyrone, I'm gonna kill you!'

'I was hungry, Ma!'

'For fuk's sake, what am I gonna do now? We can't have a party wit no food! I'm gonna have to order from de Hai Wun.'

Me ma snorts. 'Right, an' how exactly are you goin' to pay for that?' she says.

Den a voice behind me laughs an' says, 'Sure I'll look after de Chinese, it's de least I can do, wha'?'

I turn around an' it's me fukin' da. He comes over an' gives me a giant hug, den turns an' looks at me ma.

'Nice to see ye, Betty,' he says noddin' at hur. I can't believe what I'm seein'. Me ma looks like hur face is about to fall off wit de shock. Den dis young fordin wan walks up behind him an' kisses him on de cheek. He's after bringin' his fukin' prozzy wit him!

'This is Ling Ling, me fiancée,' he says.

'Hello! So very nice to meet you all!' she says wit a massive grin on hur face.

Mudder of Jaysus, me da is after gettin' engaged to yer wan. She has a mahoosive ring an' all. I'm standin' der waitin' for me ma to go ballistic – hur eye is twitchin' like it's about to pop out of hur skull – but she just polishes off hur sherry an' nods.

'I'm goin' to go make sure that everyone is doing okay. The place is really startin' to fill up now,' she says, an' she walks off, wobblin' a bit.

Whitto an' Jazzo come leggin' it over wit me angles an' dey all give me da a hug.

'Don't yiz look de part, wha'!' he says twirlin' de girls around, an' he gives dem each a Communion card. 'Me two gorgeous princesses!'

Whitto leans in to me an' whispers in me ear, 'I can't believe he brought fukin' Bling Bling or whatever hur bleedin' name is.'

'Isn't it gas? Ma's goin' to freak out wit hur here!'

'Yeah, well, speakin' of people bein' here dat ye don't want here, oul Prik Feechurs is just after comin' in wit his Garda escorts!'

I sweyour to fuk, me jaw nearly hits de floor. I run over to de door an' pull him to one side, de escorts eyeballin' me de whole time.

'Heyour, ye got to be in de church, now why aren't ye back in de Joy?' I ask. He tells me to back off, dat it's Ri Ri's day an' she's his princess too, an' dat dey're only lettin' him stay der for an hour in anyways. I remember what me ma said an' take a deep breath.

'Fine,' I say, 'but ye fukin' better be gone in an hour, or I'll be trunnin' ye out meself!'

Everyone settles down, an' for a while der's no more drama. De music is pumpin', everyone's up dancin' an' de WKDs are goin' down a fukin' treat. Everyting is just how I wanted.

Me da an' Bling Bling walk in wit massive bags of curdy an' chips an chicken balls an' everyone cheers. Fukin' nice wan! Outta nowhere me ma pops up beside me. She has anudder sherry in hur hand an' I sweyour to Jaysus I tink she's locked.

'I can't believe he brought that … that … trash with him! To *my* granddaughter's Communion!' she says, slurrin' hur words an' all. De fukin' cheek of hur!

'Say what ye want about Bling Bling, but d'ye see how happy Da is?' I say. 'He doesn't have to put up wit you moanin' an whingin' outta ye anymore an' he's delighra. Yer always fukin' interferin' an' always complainin', stickin' yer nose in where yer not wanted an' passin' comment, an' d'ye know what'? We're all fukin' sick of ye!'

Me ma turns around an' looks me in de eye for a second, den she gives me de most almighty fukin' wallop across de face. I stagger backwards an' grab me face

'What de fuk was dat for?' I say, rubbin' me cheek. Mudder of Jaysus, it's stingin' like mad.

'For bein' a cruel daughter … and a bad mother … and a horrible, horrible person!'

The whole room is starin' at us an' de music is after stoppin'. I serdiously can't believe what she just said to me! Me eyes are waterin' from de shock of de slap an' I'm actually speechless. Den Tiffo an' Harley come runnin' over an' dey help me over to de bar, as far away from me ma as possible.

'Relax, Hun,' Tiffo says. 'Yer ma's locked, an' she's pissed off dat yer da walked in wit fukin' 3-in-1 over der. Don't take it personal. She doesn't mean any of it!' An' she starts tryin' to stick two ice cubes from hur drink on me face.

'Get de fuk off me wit yer ice!'

Harley puts his arm around me. 'Tiffo is right. Dat was out of order an' all, but for now just leave it be, for Ri Ri's sake. Just leave it go, okay? Don't let all of dis ruin hur big day.'

I suppose dey have a point. Dis is me princess of power's big day after all, an' it shud be all about hur. Just keep tinkin' dat, Hun, I'm sayin' to meself. Just keep tinkin' dat.

All of a sudden one of de guards comes roarin' out of de jacks.

'He's gone! He's climbed out the window! Radio for backup!' an' de two escorts go leggin' it down de stairs.

So Prik Feechurs is after doin' a runner from de pigs! I can't say I'm surprised, de man's as tik as a fukin' plank.

I go into de jacks where all de commotion is – de pig let him use de cubicle wit de big fukin' window in it, de dopey basturd. Ri Ri comes over to me lookin' confused.

'Ma, where's me da gone?'

'He had to leave an' I don't tink he'll be back, me li'l princess of power.'

'Ah Ma, dat's not fair. I only saw him for a while.'

'Well, look at Jazzo, hur da didn't even show up. So yer lucky dat yours did for a while, right? An' yer granda is here too. Isn't dat right?'

'Yeah, I s'pose so.'

'An' d'ye know what else?'

'Wha'?'

'Der's curdy sauce, chicken balls, fried rice an' chips on de bar! Yer granda an' Bling Bling went to de Hai Wun.'

'Ah Ma, dat's deadly, I'm bleedin' starvin'! Can I have anudder bottle of red lemo?'

'Anyting ye want, me li'l princess, it's yer big day! Just don't get any curdy sauce on yer dress or I'll bate ye.'

We have a hug an' go back to de party. Everyone is millin' into de Chinese. Me da picked up a couple of batch loaves an' all so everyone cud make chip sambos. He even kept me de heel! De party starts to wind down after everyone's eaten 'til eventually we're de last ones standin'. An' of course, we have an oul sing-song after Dave packs up an' does a legger. I don't tink I'll be seein' him again. He had a nice arse on him but he was bleedin' terrified of me, an' I need a man who can handle de Hunzo charm!

At de end of de party I find me ma in de jacks snifflin' an' dabbin' hur eyes wit a bit of tissue. She's a total fukin' head-wreck, but at de end of de day she's still me ma, an' I tink we need to try an' call a truce. I know how she feels wit me da an' Bling Bling, too. It's de same way I felt when I found out Prik Feechurs was stickin' his mickey in every young wan in de village. I was fukin' livid.

'Ma, listen, I'm sorry for what I said earlier. I was bein' a kunt.'

'Jesus Hun, will you stop sayin' that word!'

'Sorry, Ma. I was bein' a geebag earlier.'

'I'm sorry too, I shouldn't have hit you like that,' she says, lookin' at me out of de corner of hur eye. 'Just when I saw yer father with that young wan I was very ... I just felt ...'

'It's alright, Ma, I know how ye feel.' Der's silence for a few seconds an' it's real awkward. Den I say, 'Ye did a great job of everyting for de Communion an' it all turned out deadly. So, eh ... can we have a truce? Whad'ye say?'

She turns around den an' gives me a kind of half-hug. Me ma doesn't really hug anyone udder dan hur grandchislers, but it's de best hug she's given me in years. I don't do all dat soppy shite, but I hug hur back, an' it makes me happy.

Robby comes upstairs to trun us out an' we say see ye after to me da an' Bling Bling.

He promises to make more of an effort to see me an' me angles, an' we even get an invite for dinner at Bling Bling's gaff in a couple of weeks. Sounds good to me – I'm presumin' she'll be makin' curdy chips, seein' as it's hur national dish. Gerrup de yard!

De next day Whitto, Jazzo an' me ma come over to de gaff an' Jazzo an' Ri Ri open der cards an' presents. De li'l kunts made an absolute fortune! We order from de chipper for a change, an' it's snack boxes all round wit red lemo an' a few garlic mayos. Fukin' nice wan. Ty Ty of course orders a Dinner Box, de hungry pig feechurs.

I get a call dat night sayin' dat Prik Feechurs was caught by de pigs. De dope went to hide in his ma's gaff. Is he for fukin' real? In anyways, I promise me li'l princess dat I'll bring hur to see him more often now he's safely back in de Joy. Ty Ty even says he'll start comin' wit us. De li'l hunga knows der's a Mickey Dee's around de corner.

Ye can say what ye want about me as a mudder, if yer a nosey pass-remarkibel, but der's nothin' I wudn't do for me li'l angles. Dey might be basturds sometimes, but dey're *my* basturds. Dey're me world an' me everyting, an I wudn't change dem for all de curdy chips in Chineseland!

Faycebuk Status Update

Hun me angles r me wurld n i wud do anything 4 dem. i had de best day wit me prince n princess n all me friends n family. yizzer de best friends n family i cud ask 4 even me ma wasint as much ov a bitch 2dey ha ha. luv yiz all ♡ ♡ xxx

Like - Comment - Share 👍2 💬6

Harley luv ye hun. ri ri lukd masso x

Hun all tanks 2 u ye lil ride ♡

Whitto it was a gr8 day xx

Hun so troo ♡

Betty DID.YOU.JUST.CALL.ME.A.BITCH

Hun ma how de fuk did u get on my faycebuk? ♡

FOLLOW IRELAND'S FAVOURITE
MICKEY MONEY HUN AT

www.facebook.com/hopeurokhun